LAWLESS LITTER

PET WHISPERER P.I.
BOOK 11

MOLLY FITZ

Editor: Jennifer Lopez, Mistress with the Red Pen
Proofreader: Jasmine Jordan
Cover: Lou Harper, Cover Affairs

PO Box 873543
Wasilla, AK 99687

This is a work of fiction. Names, characters, organizations, places, events, and incidents are either products of the author's imagination or are used fictitiously. Any resemblance to actual persons, living or dead, or actual events is purely coincidental.

ABOUT THIS BOOK

It's kittens for Octo-Cat when an orphaned litter shows up at our doorstep. And although the needy litter may be cute, the deadly mystery they bring with them is anything but.

Charles has been hinting at a big surprise he's planned for our first Valentine's Day together, but the arrival of the kittens quickly changes everything. Now he's helping me figure out who put the babies on my porch and why their paws are covered in blood.

Meanwhile Octo-Cat is left to play babysitter to the unruly brood while we investigate, and he's none too happy about it.

Right, so all we have to do is keep the kittens safe, solve their mystery, find forever homes for them, and try to find a way to salvage Valentine's Day. That shouldn't be *too* impossible...

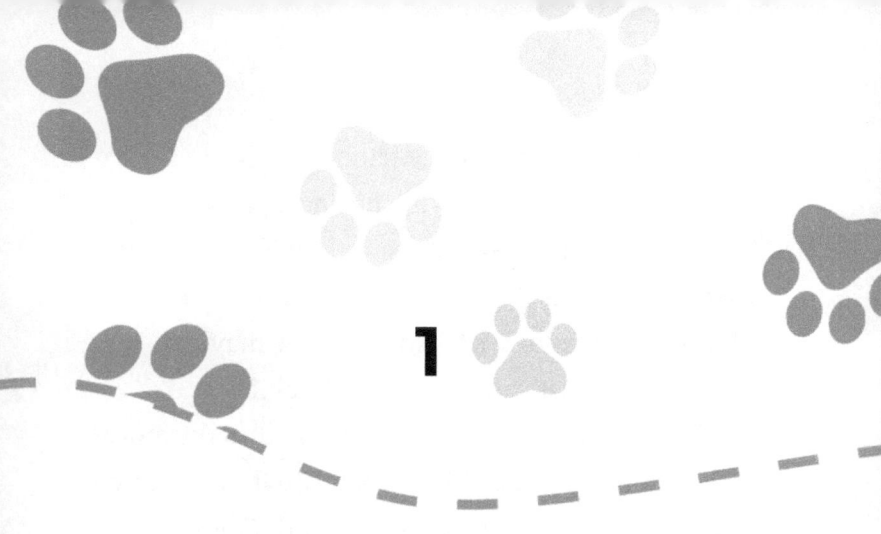

H i, my name's Angie Russo. I used to be a paralegal, but now I'm a full-time private investigator... well, at least in theory.

We only get about one case per month, and they only sometimes pay. Luckily, my cat came with a very generous trust fund from his previous owner, which solves at least one major problem.

Oh, also, my cat talks.

Not to everyone, though.

Just me.

Considering his constant stream of criticism and unwanted life advice, I'm sure he wouldn't have the time to talk to anyone else even if he were able.

Did I mention he's my partner?

No, not like that. He's my *business* partner.

My romantic partner is a handsome, brainy, sweet, and considerate attorney by the name of Charles Longfellow, III. And while I may call him "Sweetie," my cat calls him "UpChuck."

I'll probably have to cave soon and make a deal with Mr. Kitty to get him to stop that. Valentine's Day is just around the corner, and I don't want anything to ruin it for us.

Besides, Octo-Cat should be busy with his own date that night. He and his long-distance girlfriend, former show cat Grizabella, are as in love as any two cats could be. I should know, because he's constantly lording it over in front of me, saying how much better his relationship is than mine.

Cats, am I right?

Well, I also have a dog—a little rescue Chihuahua named Paisley. She technically belongs to my nan, but we all live together.

Paisley is sweet like a double scoop of double fudge ice cream covered in sprinkles and chocolate sauce. Sometimes she's too optimistic about people's intentions, which means she's not exactly the best crime-solving partner.

Nan, on the other hand, uses all her varied life

experience to solve our cases in the most unusual way possible. As a former Broadway actress, she's all about costumes, accents, and general over-the-topness.

Boy, do I love her for it.

Speaking of love, I have a bit of a love-hate relationship with the raccoon who lives in my back yard. His name is Pringle and he has zero boundaries. Not too long ago, he uncovered a long-buried family secret by snooping around the attic—we still haven't fully resolved that one—but he also kind of saved my life a couple weeks ago. I guess that makes us even.

As a thank-you, I now allow him to come into the house whenever he pleases. And he "pleases" quite often. Our grocery bill has risen precipitously. Meanwhile, Pringle is beginning to resemble a literal fuzz ball with all the junk food he puts away on a daily basis.

Sometimes I wish I'd never had that near-death experience that left me with my ability to talk to animals, but then I remember all the amazing things I've gained in life since then. Don't tell him, but the greatest of those things is my friendship with Octo-Cat.

Sure, he only sometimes shows me affection,

but when he does it's enough to keep a smile on my face all day.

That brings us to today.

It's been T-minus six days since my cat deigned to let me pet him. My parents have been on a glamorous Alaskan cruise for the past three days, and I have had no cases since investigating the mayor's missing golden retriever last month.

All this downtime has got me wondering whether I should take up a hobby while I wait for the next big case to land in my lap. I have tried advertising, but that's mostly been a bust. So what else can I really do?

Ugh.

Maybe I should go back to school and finally work toward a bachelor's degree in Criminal Justice or something.

I have seven associate degrees, because I've always loved learning too much to commit to any one field for four whole years. But now that I'm a PI, I can't picture any other life for me. Would a degree help bolster the confidence of potential clients?

Or maybe someday I could officially join the police force and work as a salaried detective? Would they let me forgo a human partner in favor of my cat?

Hmm. If not, that might be a deal-breaker.

So many options, but none of them are just right.

I'm pretty sure I know what I need to do, and it's the one thing I've been trying so desperately to avoid ever since I got started.

My boyfriend Charles is the senior partner at his law firm and has offered on more than one occasion to hire me through the firm to help with cases. Sure, Charles was a good boss while I worked for him as a paralegal—in fact, that's how we first met and became friends.

But our relationship has evolved so much since then, and I'm worried it might hurt the good thing we have going together. Also, returning to the law firm feels like a giant step back even if my job title would change.

I guess what I'm trying to tell you is that I just don't know what to do.

Maybe the cat would be willing to decide for me...

* * *

Octo-Cat regarded me with a piteous look. He flicked his tail and knocked a bottle of painkillers from the nightstand on which he was perched. "See, this right here. *This* is why you need me."

I'd planned to do a little reading before tucking in for the night, but the two of us had gotten to talking about my conundrum and—as expected—the tabby had no shortage of opinions.

"Think about it," he continued, swinging the tip of his tail like a metronome. "Everything you have is because of me. House. Job. Boyfriend. Need I go on?"

I swallowed down my comeback. Sad to say, he was right. I hated that he was right.

"So what should I do?" I asked with wide eyes.

"Isn't it obvious?" He narrowed his eyes at me, then groaned. "Oh, right. Forgot who I was talking to for a moment there."

I resisted the urge to pick him up and carry him out into the hall so that I could shut the door between us and finally get some peace.

Octo-Cat, however, continued his lecture unaware of just how painfully it was being received. "You should take the work from UpChuck. *Duh.*"

"Don't call him that," I mumbled.

He rolled his large amber eyes. "You need more

experience and references, and he's offering to help you get those. It's not just *you* you have to think about here."

I bit my thumbnail and sighed. "Okay," I said simply. "I'll talk to him tomorrow then."

My tabby seemed pleased with this conclusion. "Now are there any other parts of your life that you need me to fix for you tonight, or can I go about my nightly duties?"

"What nightly duties?" This was the first I'd heard of them, and while Octo-Cat *did* help solve cases, he did precious little else with his days. Could the nights really be all that different?

"Oh, you know. Keeping my favorite spot on the couch warm. Walking over all the counters and tables to make sure they're still sturdy. Protecting the house from ghosts. Watching the—"

"Wait. Go back a second there. Ghosts?"

He glared at me as if I should have known better than to interrupt his soliloquy. "Yes. Didn't you know? Only cats can see them."

I studied him for a second in an attempt to figure out whether he was being serious, but he just stared at me blankly, giving absolutely nothing away.

"Are ghosts really *real?*" I squeaked. I knew I

had something of a magical ability, but I had a hard time believing that those fairytale supernatural creatures walked among us.

My cat yawned, and his smelly tuna breath hit me full-on in the face. "Guess you'll never know," he said flippantly before jumping off the side table and trotting out of the room.

Ghosts? *Huh.*

Something told me I might not sleep so well that night.

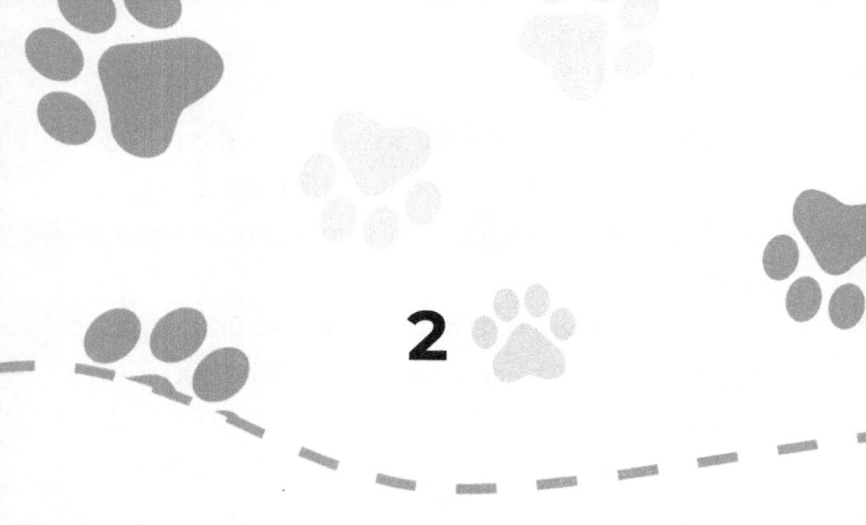

2

Saturday had arrived, and I was looking forward to sleeping in and waking up extra refreshed.

Nan, however, had other plans. She breezed into my room bright and early, carrying a coffee mug so full I had to wonder how she kept from spilling. "Rise and shine!" she sang, beaming at me from her spot next to my bed.

I wiped the sleep from my eyes and pulled myself into a sitting position. The wooden spindles of my old-fashioned headboard dug into my back, offering me a rather rude awakening, indeed.

Nan pressed the coffee mug into my hands. Some of the hot liquid escaped, sloshing over the side of the cup and onto my comforter.

That was when Paisley arrived. "Good morning, Mommy!" she barked before belting out a spirited rendition of some happy little nursery rhyme about a doggie in a window.

It was all way too much noise first thing in the morning, and I'd never been a morning person to begin with.

"What do you want?" I snapped, perhaps a bit too unkindly.

Nan narrowed her eyes at me. "Don't sass me, dear. I'm headed out for my new booty boot camp class in a few minutes."

"Thanks for asking, but I'm not interested," I groaned, attempting to take a sip of the coffee but spilling again.

My grandmother shook her head. "Good. Because I didn't invite you. I was lucky to get the one spot I did. This class usually has a six-month waitlist, but they somehow managed to squeeze me in at the last minute."

"Then what do you need?" I asked from behind the steaming mug.

She raised both arms and motioned toward me. "To give you that."

I eyed my coffee and nodded my thanks. Nan always brewed it for me, given my well-documented fear of coffee makers. It may seem silly, but I'd just never been able to look at them the same after my near-death experience last year. Of course I'd tried other forms of caffeine, but none sated my addiction quite like a good old-fashioned cup of joe.

"Have fun at class," I said sweetly, feeling guilty now for having snapped earlier.

Nan lifted her arms in front of her at shoulder height, then did a quick dip and squat. "I won't," she said with a grin. "That's the point. Beauty through pain."

"You're already beautiful, Nan," I muttered. Even though I'd taken up jogging with Nan a few days a week, she was still in far better shape than me—and, wrinkled or not, her body showed it.

She turned and shook her bottom, which was clad in pink velour sweatpants. "I'm looking to tighten and tone. If Grant ever gets around to officially asking me out, I want to be ready."

I shuddered at the thought. While I was happy that my grandmother had found a close friend in Mr. Grant Gable, I definitely didn't want to think about how said friendship might involve her needing a tight and toned bottom.

"Well, I'm off!" Nan trilled, heading back out my bedroom door with Paisley yapping at her heels.

I sat sipping my coffee and thinking about what I wanted to accomplish with my day. Saturdays used to be my favorite, but now that I was self-employed every day was both a work day and a vacation—not a good vacation, but rather the kind that happened when I didn't have enough to keep me busy on the job.

Sigh.

"Morning, shrimpy." Octo-Cat appeared in the doorway seeming rather pleased with himself.

I raised one quizzical brow. "Why shrimpy?"

"Why not? Humans call each other sweetie, sugar, and honey, so I figured I'd try calling you after a food *I* like."

Given that my cat loved shrimp to an inhuman degree, I was very touched—and also glad that no one else could hear him calling me this strange new nickname.

A smile spread between his whiskers as Octo-Cat luxuriated in a long sunbeam that had stretched lazily across the bedroom floor. He looked really happy.

...too happy.

"May I help you with something?" I asked, suddenly very suspicious.

He did a crazy-looking cat yoga pose and then

jumped up onto the bed beside me. "I thought you'd never ask."

Uh-oh.

"Since we don't have any active cases right now, I figured this would be a good time for you to drive me to Grizabella's for a visit."

I almost choked in shock. "But she lives in Colorado. That's a really long car ride. And besides, how would I explain such a trip to her owner?"

"Christine is *not* her owner," my cat said emphatically. "We both know the cat's always the one in charge."

"Fair point."

Octo-Cat shook his head in disappointment, then whipped his face back toward me. A sneaky smile stretched from furry cheek to furry cheek. "As for Christine, I'm sure you'll think of something during the long drive over."

His piece said, the tabby lifted his tail high, then turned to leave.

"Wait," I called before he'd made his exit.

Octo-Cat peeked back over his shoulder. "Yes?"

"I don't think we can manage a trip to see Grizabella right now."

"Why not? It's not like you have any work to do."

He had me there. "I just don't think—"

"No, it has nothing to do with thinking. The truth is *you don't want to,* but next Friday is Valentine's Day and I haven't seen my gorgeous Grizz since Thanksgiving week."

I sat higher in bed, hoping the change in posture might render me more convincing in my deceit. I supported Octo-Cat's relationship and wanted him to be happy, but this request was simply ridiculous.

"Yeah, it's Valentine's Day!" I practically shouted. "I already have plans with Charles."

"No, you don't."

"How do you know I don't?"

He heaved a giant breath. "When you're sleeping, Pringle goes through your phone and reads everything to me."

My heart dropped right into my stomach. "WHAT?! What's *everything?*"

He smirked. "You know, texts, emails, status updates, the works. And neither you nor UpChuck has mentioned any Valentine's Day plans."

I was stuck, stuck, so hopelessly stuck... but also very angry now. "You can't just look at my private stuff!"

Octo-Cat chuckled. "You're my human. There shouldn't be any secrets between us."

And with that he left.

I took another sip from my mug, but by now the coffee had grown cold. As much as I loved my bossy, overbearing feline, I just couldn't rationalize an impromptu cross-country trip, especially when his girlfriend's human had no idea I could talk to cats.

I needed to find a way out of this.

And I probably needed to change the passcode on my phone, too.

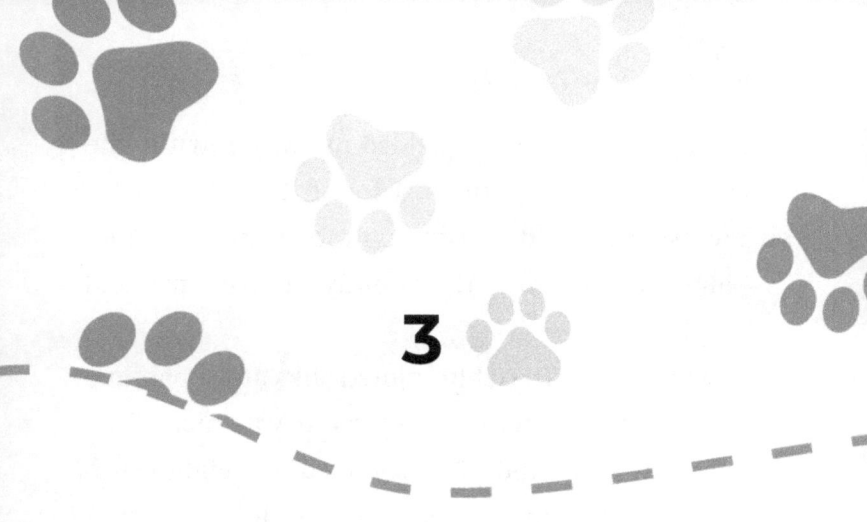

3

As much as I'd have liked to go back to sleep, the fresh coffee stains covering a good portion of my comforter made that inadvisable. Besides, I didn't need to lend any credence to Octo-Cat's argument that I should take him to see his Internet girlfriend all the way over in Colorado. He already claimed I did nothing with my days, and sleeping through this one would prove that theory of his.

Hmm.

Maybe I could trick him with a made-up case to keep us both busy until he found a new idea to obsess over. Then again, he wasn't the easiest cat in the world to fool. I could find a legitimate case before next Friday. Couldn't I?

Already at a loss, I padded my way down to the second floor. Once there, I found Octo-Cat in his new bedroom, sitting right on top of the giant 140-gallon aquarium I'd recently caved in and bought him.

Outfitted with richly colored silks and a baroque decorating scheme, my cat's room was nicer than mine. It also kind of resembled an eighteenth-century Parisian brothel—or at least what I assumed one might look like.

An accurate comparison or not, I felt immensely out of place whenever I entered, which meant I mostly gave Octo-Cat his privacy. Not that he ever returned the favor.

Still, someone needed to feed his fish—and it was better if that someone didn't find herself tempted to eat them every time the lid to their tank was opened.

"I've told you I can handle it," my cat groused when I grabbed the canister of food flakes and twisted off the top.

I shrugged off his argument. "Yeah. I'm not in the habit of inviting disaster into my home."

"*My* home," he corrected with an irritated sniff. "And what are you talking about? *Disaster* is basically your middle name."

"Maybe. But I doubt your fish would appreciate you sticking your paws into the tank and batting at them with those sharp little claws of yours."

Octo-Cat jumped off the tank and raised a paw to his chest. "Who are you calling *little?* I am deeply offended, and so are they. My fish have names, and I'll thank you to use them."

Even though I regularly talked to pets and forest animals, I'd never once heard Octo-Cat's fish utter anything other than "blub, blub." Was he simply pulling my leg about this? Then again, if other animals could talk, why wouldn't fish be able to as well?

Still pondering this, I sprinkled the food into their tank and quickly closed the lid to avoid any kitty shenanigans.

When Octo-Cat jumped back on top to watch them through the tiny opening for the water filter in the back, I decided to ask for a little clarification on the matter. "What are they?"

"They're fish, genius."

I met his eyeroll with one of my own. "Of course, they're fish. But you mentioned they have names. Right? So, tell me, what are they?"

He hopped back onto the floor and sat at my

side, his eyes trailing the largest fish as it swam idly about the tank. "See, that big orange one? That's Tasty."

"Uh-huh. What about the striped one?"

He smiled and shifted his gaze to the aforementioned fish. "That's Delicious."

I was beginning to see a pattern here but continued to listen until all the fish had been named—among them were Yummy, Scrumptious, and Appi-teaser. My guess was he'd seen a few too many commercials for a certain restaurant chain leading to the made-up name of that last one.

I didn't point this out, though.

Instead I shook my head and said, "I'm not letting you eat your fish. They're supposed to be your pets."

"Angela," he said, aghast. "Who says I want to eat them?"

"You—" I began but was cut off by the merry chime of the doorbell. I didn't recognize the tune since Nan had recently changed it. It definitely had an upbeat doo-wop vibe about it, but I wasn't particularly fluent in that era of music.

"We'll finish this later," I promised the tabby before racing down the stairs.

Upon pulling the door open, I found my other half, Charles, waiting on the front porch with a giant grin on his face. He immediately wrapped his arms around my waist and pulled me in for a kiss.

"Gag. Get a room," Octo-Cat spat as he finished descending the stairs.

I chuckled as Charles and I finished our greeting.

"Great idea. We'll use yours," I told the mean kitty.

Charles bunched his eyebrows in confusion. "Use my *what?* Oh, right. You were talking to the cat, weren't you?"

"Sorry. He's just being bratty, but I'm focused on you now." I flushed and tucked a fallen strand of hair behind my ear. Sometimes I forgot that others could only hear one side of my animal conversations. "What's with the early-morning surprise?"

"I thought we could spend the day together, if that's all right with you."

"That's perfect with me." I gave him another long, lingering kiss.

Octo-Cat walked by, then stopped and pretended to retch—except that part-way through his performance, his faked motions led to a very real need to empty his stomach.

"Gross!" I cried when the puddle of puke landed just a few inches from my left foot.

"You're telling me," Octo-Cat responded before trotting into the kitchen and leaving me to clean his mess.

"Well, that's romantic," Charles quipped with a goofy laugh.

"Isn't it just?" I carefully turned away and grabbed the cleaning spray and a roll of paper towels from our coat closet.

"It's okay if today's not perfect," Charles assured me, accepting the dirty bunch of used paper towels from me. "Today's just Saturday. It's next Friday that's important."

"What do you—?" I stopped when I noticed Charles's face had crumpled into a frown. "Valentine's Day, yes. I'm really excited."

I wasn't a doting romantic, but I loved that Charles was.

"This will be our first one together, and I want to make sure it's special." He sprinted toward the kitchen to dump the soiled towels into the trash.

"Okay. What should we do?" I asked with an innocent smile as he jogged back.

"Don't worry. I've got it all planned out."

"Great. Tell me about it."

"Nope. It's a surprise." Something flashed in his eyes that made my stomach fill with butterflies, both because I loved Charles and because I had a tendency to fear the unknown.

"Just so long as you're not planning to propose," I joked before I could stop myself.

Charles's face fell again. This time my heart sped to a million beats per minute—or somewhere thereabouts.

"Oh," I said when nothing better came to mind.

My boyfriend reached his hand up to cup the back of his neck and averted his gaze toward the floor. "Um, I was going to wait until the big day, but..." His words trailed off as he sunk to the floor, took a knee, and then looked back up at me with bright, hopeful eyes.

"Charles, I..." I *what?* What could I possibly say to this?

I loved him. I'd committed to him. But I didn't want to get married just yet. Not until I had my life and business in better working order.

He licked his lips, took my hand in his, and then burst out laughing. "Just kidding!"

Octo-Cat guffawed with laughter as he passed by yet again. "Ha! Maybe UpChuck's not so bad, after all," he muttered to himself.

And as much as I hated that cat's snarky comments about my boyfriend, I hated the idea of them teaming up against me even more.

Luckily, Charles had no idea what Octo-Cat had just said.

I wouldn't be telling him, either.

4

Charles brewed a fresh pot of coffee for us while I warmed Nan's latest batch of homemade muffins in the microwave.

"Do you really have the full day free?" I asked again in disbelief.

"Not free," he corrected, pulling his favorite butterscotch-flavored creamer from the fridge and sending a wide grin my way. "I'm spending it with you."

"It's just you don't usually get a half day off, let alone a full one."

"Well, I'm making some changes at the firm to help me focus on what's most important."

"There's a lot to be said for work-life balance. I

kind of have the opposite problem. Too much life and not enough work."

"Hmm. Then maybe we should meet in the middle." He winked suggestively, making me blush all over again.

"Excuse me," Octo-Cat bellowed as he joined us in the kitchen and stared down into his half-empty water dish.

I turned to face him. "Yes, your royal highness?"

"Oh, I like that," the tabby drawled as he twitched his tail in thought. "It's about time you referred to me properly."

"I didn't mean..." I began, then stopped myself. If I wanted to actually spend the day with Charles, I'd need to avoid unnecessary arguments with Octo-Cat in the meantime.

"What is it?" I asked amicably. The sooner I could satisfy his demands, the sooner I'd have some much-needed quality time with Charles—some much needed and *uninterrupted* quality time.

"I need you to bring my iPad into the mid-morning sunspot. I have a call planned with Grizabella, and I can't be late."

"Okay, give me a second," I said over the beeping of the microwave.

"I don't need it a second from now. I need it

now." Octo-Cat stomped one of his front feet and glared at me with those strangely glowing eyes of his. "I'm going to tell her about our visit next week. I can't wait to see the look on that beautiful face of hers when she finds out—"

"No," I interrupted, perhaps a bit too emphatically.

My cat's head shot back as though he'd been slapped. "What do you mean *no?*"

Apparently I didn't say this word enough, given that Octo-Cat seemed to have forgotten what it meant or that it was ever a possible answer to something he wanted. *Uh-oh.* I needed to think fast before he could either outwit or guilt-trip me into doing his bidding.

"I, um... I was just talking with Charles, and you were right. He does have work for us at the firm. We can't leave town, because we need to get started bright and early Monday morning."

He lifted his tail and bent it to resemble a question mark. "Is that so?"

I jabbed Charles in the ribs, and he nodded despite not knowing what was going on.

"Hmm, I guess that's good," Octo-Cat conceded a moment later. "I've always thought St. Patrick's

Day was far more romantic, anyway. Green is a much nicer color than pink or red, and who doesn't like pots of gold?"

I laughed nervously. "Yeah. Good point."

He nodded and glanced toward the living room. "You can have the inferior romantic holiday then. Now about that thing I needed."

Even if I hadn't claimed an outright victory, at least I'd managed to delay the problematic road trip for another month. That was pretty good for a morning's work. "Right. I'll go get your iPad for you."

"What was that all about?" Charles asked after I'd returned.

"Shhh," I hissed. "He can still hear you."

Charles leaned in close and pressed his lips to my ear. "You're cute when you're arguing with your cat. You know that?"

My knees turned to Jell-O as he traced kisses down my neck. "Stop that, you."

Charles chuckled as he pulled away.

While he finished fixing our coffee, I grabbed my phone from my pocket and typed out a text.

Charles's pocket buzzed a moment later. "What the—? It's from you?"

I widened my eyes and motioned toward his pocket. Yes, it was silly to text when we were standing in the same room, but I didn't want to risk Octo-Cat overhearing what I needed to say.

My boyfriend's eyes trailed down the screen and his lips moved as he read.

I need you to assign a case for us. Even if it's fake, just something to keep us busy. Otherwise he's going to force me to drive him out to Colorado.

He snorted and typed back, *What's wrong with Colorado?*

I'll miss V-Day.

Can't have that, he typed, then jammed his phone back into his back pocket and wrapped me in his arms.

"Thank you," I whispered against his shoulder.

That was when a projectile thumped into the back of my head.

I spun on my heels, not at all surprised to see Pringle the raccoon standing nearby, his Nerf gun still pointed straight at me.

"You're not supposed to use that on me," I reminded him with a groan.

"How else was I supposed to get your attention away from lover boy?" The masked nuisance crossed his arms but continued to shoot darts at me with those dark, beady eyes of his.

"What do you need?" And why were my animals constantly inserting themselves into my love life? I hardly got any time with Charles as it was. The last thing I needed was to play human servant to the furry creatures all day. Paisley, at least, was busy with Nan, but that didn't help me with the ones who were still here.

Pringle widened his eyes and tsked. "Watch the attitude, toots. I come in peace."

"That's a fine thing to say when you literally just shot me."

Pringle chittered happily. "Yeah, that was pretty good. Wasn't it?"

I tapped my foot, refusing to say anything more until he just came out with whatever it was he needed. The sooner he told me, the sooner he could be on his way.

The raccoon dropped to all fours and raced back through the living room. "I have something important to show you. C'mon!" he cried. "Follow me!"

"What does he want?" Charles asked with one suspicious eyebrow raised.

"No idea. Let's go up to my bedroom and lock the door."

He raised the other eyebrow. "Not that I don't like how you think, but we should probably find out what has him so worked up."

I grabbed the plate of muffins and one of the coffee mugs. "Not interested. Now let's go."

Unfortunately, Pringle intercepted me just as I reached the stairs. "And just where do you think you're going?" he demanded before shooting a foam dart into each of my kneecaps.

"Ouch! Stop it!"

He shot another dart at my face. "I'll stop when you come out to the porch with me."

"What's on the porch?" I asked with a sigh.

He landed a shot near my bellybutton.

I growled in frustration. "You want me to go the porch? Then give me that gun. You've lost Nerf privileges for the rest of the year as far as I'm concerned."

Pringle bared his teeth and hissed, reminding me that no matter how well he spoke, he was still very much a wild animal. "Touch Carla and you'll deserve what happens to you next."

"Enough with the theatrics." Charles pushed past us and flung open the door.

"See!" the raccoon shouted in indignation as our

eyes fell upon the bloody scene waiting on the front porch. He bolted past us and leaped off the porch.

"It's your problem now!" he called as he disappeared around the side of the house.

And, yes, a problem it most definitely was.

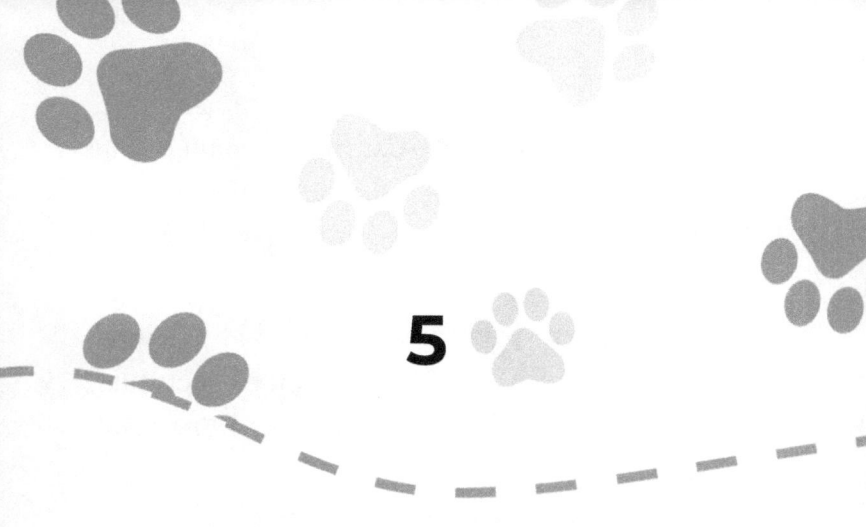

5

"Mamamamamamamama!" one of the babies cried when we stepped out onto the porch. Her feet were covered in blood, but she didn't seem to be in pain.

Her brothers and sisters clambered over her in an attempt to break free of the battered cardboard box they'd been crammed into.

"Are those...?" Charles let his voice trail off.

I nodded to confirm. "An abandoned litter of kittens."

Octo-Cat marched past us both. "What's all this noise? I'm trying to speak with Grizabella and—"

A chorus of excited mews rose up to interrupt him. "Daddy!"

I glanced toward Octo-Cat in just enough time to see his already large eyes grow wide in horror.

He coughed and took a fearful step back. "No, it can't be. The vet stole my cathood at least..."

He lifted a paw and extracted his claws, counting until he was satisfied with the conclusion. "At least four years ago. These... These *things* can't be mine."

"Daddy!" the kittens chorused again.

"It's impossible," Octo-Cat insisted, stepping forward to sniff at the box. "And besides, they look nothing like me."

They, in fact, looked very much like him with the same golden eyes and the same brown tabby coats. The only difference was that their fur was already longer than his. Based on my limited experience as a crazy cat lady, I guessed that this was a litter of Maine Coons. Fitting, given that we lived in Maine and that Octo-Cat liked to claim this particular breed as part of his proud heritage.

The kittens rushed to one side of the box in an effort to get close to the grown-up feline, and in so doing, knocked the box over. Free at last, they rushed up to my cat and began to rub affectionately against him.

"Oh, great! Now they got this red sticky stuff all

over me, too," he moaned but surprisingly made no move to back away.

Pringle reappeared then. Once on the porch, he started scooping up kittens and tucking them into his armpits. "How much do you think these guys are worth on the web market?"

"No," I shouted. "Both of you stop! Nobody's accusing you of being their father," I informed my tedious tabby. "And we are not selling them on the Internet," I growled at the handsy raccoon.

Charles placed an arm around my waist and pulled me to his side. "What are we going to do?"

"Let's start by bringing them inside and getting them cleaned up," I decided aloud. At this point, I was feeling quite thankful that Nan was out and about. If she'd been here to discover the kittens with us, I had no doubt in my mind that all five would become permanent residents of our home—and that Octo-Cat would make me suffer for it.

Charles helped me wrestle the babies back into the box, then picked it up and carried them toward the biggest of our bathrooms, the one with the claw-footed tub.

Both Octo-Cat and Pringle followed along.

Pringle no longer had his Nerf gun, so that at least offered a small measure of relief. "I'm telling you," he said in a raspy whisper. "We should be able to get at least $100 each, and with there being five kittens in all, that's like a thousand dollars."

Apparently Pringle's math wasn't as good as his reading. Given a choice, I'd have gladly flipped that the other way around.

"Go on," Octo-Cat urged, dollar signs practically popping up in his eyes. "I'm listening."

I crossed my arms and glared at the naughty animals. "That's it! If I hear any more talk of selling the kittens, I'm demolishing your tree house."

Pringle crossed his arms and glared right back at me. "Which one?"

"Both."

"You wouldn't."

"Try me."

"If I had Carla, you wouldn't be so fast to make threats."

"Is that so? Go on. Go get her then."

When Pringle raced out of the bathroom, I slammed the door shut behind him. Locked it, too, for good measure.

"It never gets old watching you interact with them." Charles chuckled as he twisted the knobs on the tub.

"Shut those off, please."

"Why? I thought we were giving the kittens a bath."

"Not like that we aren't."

I grabbed a pair of wash cloths from the linen closet, wet them both, and handed one to Charles. "They've had enough trauma for the day. Let's do it this way."

Once the little bit of water had drained from the tub, we placed the kittens inside and worked on wiping the blood and grime from each of them in turn.

"There." Charles returned the last of the kittens to the floor with triumph. "All done."

"Not quite," I whispered. Unfortunately, my whisper wasn't quite quiet enough.

"What do you mean *not quite?*" Octo-Cat, who had been watching with great interest from his perch on top of the toilet tank, questioned.

Realization flashed in his eyes a moment later. When it did, he pressed his ears back against his head and hissed. "I can wassssh myssssssself!"

"Grab him now!" I shouted to Charles.

And he made a good job of it despite the cat's violent flailing.

"This will only take a second," I promised.

"I'm not a baby," he grumped. "I don't need to be coddled by you."

"Maybe so, but you've got blood on you, too. And we need to get it off."

"I hate you," Octo-Cat growled over and over until we'd finished.

If I hadn't been every bit as miserable as him, I might have considered extending the impromptu bath just to punish him for his cruel words.

By the time Charles let him back onto the floor, he was covered in a flurry of little striped hairs that had resulted from Octo-Cat's stress-shedding.

"That wasn't so bad now. Was it, big guy?" Charles asked, attempting—and failing—to wipe some of it off.

"You better watch your back, UpChuck," my cat moaned, knowing Charles couldn't understand the threat. "Actually, *don't.* It will make my revenge that much sweeter."

I shot him a warning glance, then opened the door to let him run out.

WOMP!

No sooner had the door opened than something hit me square on the nose. And that something was one of Carla's foam darts.

"Pringle!" I screamed in frustration.

Six distinct laughs rose in the bathroom—five from the kittens whose lives we'd just saved and the last of them from my sweet, loyal, loving boyfriend.

Maybe Octo-Cat was right.

Maybe he should watch his back.

Foam or not, those darts hurt, especially considering Pringle's unforgiving aim. I needed to find a way to get that thing away from him once and for all... But first, kittens.

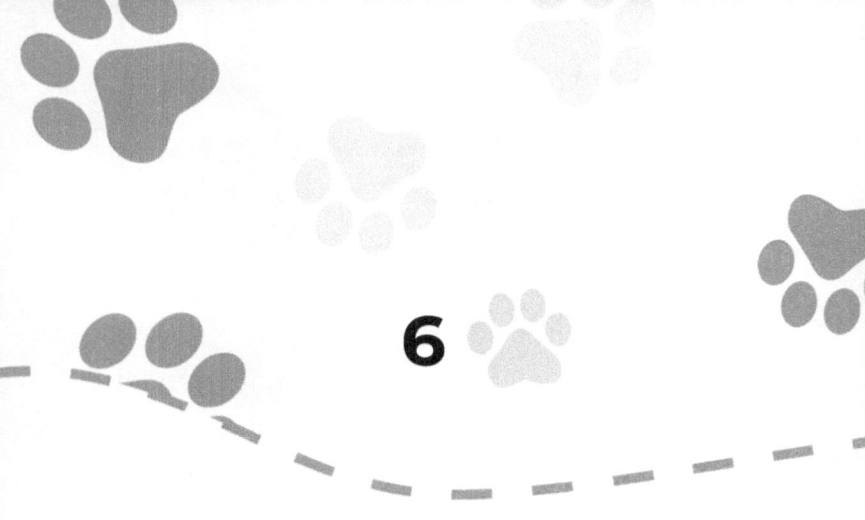

6

couldn't get the Nerf gun away from the raccoon ranger, but I did manage to chase him outside and shut the pet door tight. Hopefully now there wouldn't be any more surprises this morning.

When I returned to the bathroom, I found Charles sitting on the edge of the bath tub and holding a swaddled kitten in each arm. As much as I wasn't ready yet for kids and marriage, the scene melted my heart into a pulsing puddle of goo.

He noticed me watching him and gave me a sweet smile—so sweet I forgave him for laughing at my unpleasant run-in with Pringle's dart. "C'mon, grab some purritos, and let's head some place more comfortable."

Oh, this man definitely knew my love language.

"Let's get them settled in Octo-Cat's bedroom," I suggested, knowing that there would be heck to pay but also knowing that it was our best option on such short notice.

Somehow, I managed to juggle three swaddled kitties as we crossed the short distance to Octo-Cat's bedroom.

My cat stood waiting at the threshold, flicking his tail so violently I worried it might snap off. "Don't even think about it," he grumbled.

But I refused to be scared off. His bedroom was the safest place for the squirmy kittens. After all, it had already been thoroughly cat-proofed and there were no large pieces of furniture for them to hide under. Octo-Cat would just have to suck it up for a change.

I set my jaw firm and my gaze straight ahead as I stepped past him into the room.

He trotted after me, screaming like a banshee. "I will throw up! I'll shred the curtains! I'll go on a hunger strike. I'll—"

"I'll tell Grizabella they're yours," I countered.

He sank back. "You wouldn't."

"I know this is mildly inconvenient for you, but they're babies and they need our help. Can you please try to be civil for once in your nine lives?"

He scoffed and turned tail. "You owe me. You owe me so big, Angela," he shouted as he ran fast and far from that room.

Whatever. I could worry about him later. For now Charles and I had kittens to attend to.

After shutting the door tight, we unwrapped each kitten and set them in the middle of the carpeted floor.

"Daddy?" one of the striped kidlets asked.

Then all the others joined. "Daddy! Daddy!" they whined, becoming increasingly agitated with each syllable.

"What got them so worked up all of a sudden?" Charles laughed, failing to realize that the cries were ones of anguish and not excitement.

"They want Octo-Cat back," I explained as Charles sat with the kittens on the floor and I stood awkwardly by the doorway. "They think he's their father."

Charles laughed. "Do they?"

"Either that, or they're just calling him *Daddy*. They don't seem to know many words."

"Well, they are babies." He picked up one of the kittens and set it on his lap. "Maybe they need to learn to talk the same way humans do. Then again, I haven't heard you talk *to* them yet. Just *about* them."

"You're right." I shook my head at this oversight, then lowered myself to the floor and sat cross-legged so the kittens could approach me. "Hi, guys. My name's Angie. What are your names?"

"Want Daddy!" one of them informed me. His whiskers brushing up against my bare foot as he sniffed me. Even though the mewling fuzzballs were adorable, they were already proving to be a ridiculous amount of work.

"I'll go get him in a second, but first I was hoping you could tell me how you wound up on my porch?"

No sooner had I asked this question than the entire litter broke into hysterics—even Charles could sense their distress. He reached out to pet the nearest kitty and received a clawed swipe for his efforts.

"That settles it." I pushed myself back to my feet, careful not to make contact with any of the angry babies as I stood. "We need to get Octo-Cat."

"Something tells me he's not going to be happy about playing translator."

I giggled. "And what *something* is that? Every single past experience to date?"

Now we both laughed. It was funny because it was true.

Charles followed me out of the room, carefully shutting the kittens inside before looping his arms around my waist. "This reminds me of the first time we really got to know each other. Remember the Hayes double homicide?"

"How could I forget? But it's kind of weird that you seem to consider it a romantic memory." I spun out of his arms and headed down the stairs.

"Hey, our relationship may be a little bit different, but it's all ours," he explained, trailing behind me. "Speaking of, I can't wait for Friday. I am going to knock your socks off with my big Valentine's Day surprise."

At the bottom of the stairs, I surveyed the foyer and the living room but couldn't see Octo-Cat anywhere. Turning back to Charles, I frowned. "Either tell me now or stop teasing. You know I hate surprises."

As we headed toward the kitchen, Octo-Cat shot out from under the couch and raced away as fast as his little paws could carry him. "You hate surprises? Well, not as much as me!" he yelled while fleeing.

We gave chase. "I need your help," I called to the raging tabby. "Please. It's important."

"Not going to happen," he muttered from the safety of the litter box where he'd taken up refuge.

"Please?" I asked, sticking out my lower lip pathetically and attempting puppy eyes. I didn't expect either gesture to work, but I had nothing else at my disposal. Even when he was in a good mood, Octo-Cat made a stubborn opponent—and he was far from a good mood now.

"No," he spat.

I sighed and hung my head. "Just remember. You forced my hand."

"Where are you going?" Charles asked as I left Octo-Cat behind and headed toward the kitchen.

"Stay here and keep watch," I instructed. "I'll be right back."

After a minute or so rummaging through the junk drawer in the kitchen, I found what I needed and returned to the guys. "Last chance," I warned the cat.

"Still no. No, no, no, no, no," came my cat's reply.

That was my cue to activate the laser pointer and trace a small shaky pattern along the floor. Sure enough, Octo-Cat emerged from his safe haven to pounce at the captivating red dot. For whatever reason, it was the one thing he could never resist.

"Haha, gotcha." Charles grabbed Octo-Cat tight and held him against his chest.

Together, we headed back toward the grand staircase, ready to deliver our hissing cargo.

"I hate you," my cat told me for what must have been the hundredth time that day. And as much as I didn't like hearing that, I shook his words off.

He'd been mad at me before and he'd be mad at me again, but if we didn't help these kittens now, they may not get another chance.

7

We returned to the cat bedroom with a very unhappy Octo-Cat in tow.

The kittens, on the other hand, were ecstatic to see him again. Their once-anguished cries immediately turned to purring as they crowded around Octo-Cat and pressed their bodies to him.

"There's a reason I never had kids, you know," the poor guy wheezed, almost making me feel bad for him. Almost.

He extricated himself from the litter and went to wait by the door. "I like to be appreciated, but this is way too much for anyone."

Could have fooled me on that one. Until now, Octo-Cat had never indicated that he could receive too much love or praise—as long as each was given on *his* terms.

"They love you," I said gently.

He kept his pointed gaze on the door. "They don't even know me. Now let me out."

I had to stop myself from answering, "That's probably why they love you." Octo-Cat only enjoyed snark when he was the one giving it.

"Can I try something?" Charles asked.

I motioned for him to go ahead.

"Think back to when you were a kitten," he addressed Octo-Cat with a placating expression. Of course, he had no idea how his words were being received by the subject. "Wouldn't you have liked to have a bigger, cooler cat to help show you the way?"

Octo-Cat snorted. "And this guy is considered smart by your kind? Oh, brother."

Well, I could have told Charles that appealing to the tabby's sense of compassion would be a no-go. We needed take a harder tack. "You're not getting out of this room until we help these kittens."

"Fine. Let's help them back where they came from. To the porch!" He shifted on his paws but remained glued to the spot.

I raised one eyebrow. "Still not convinced?"

"Not in the slightest." Octo-Cat kept his nose

high in the air, refusing to look at either me or the kittens despite their continued efforts to claim his attention. They'd scrambled their way over and were now sitting in a straight line behind him, also staring at the door.

"I'm not backing down on this. But since you seem to need an extra bit of convincing, I'm going to send a text to Nan right now to see if she can help." I pulled out my phone and began typing away.

He scoffed. "Oooh, I'm shaking in my fur."

"What's Nan going to do?" Charles wondered aloud.

I smirked as I hit send. "She and Paisley are going to stop by the store on their way home from booty boot camp. I've asked her to pick up some generic brand *dry* cat food.

My cat seethed with rage. He obviously wanted to take a swipe at me, but still remained rooted to the spot in front of the door. "You wouldn't."

"Oh, but I would." I cackled like a witch. Although I hated having to resort to such measures, I also somewhat enjoyed giving my cat what was coming to him. "I've asked Nan to get store-brand crunchies for you and a new bowl for Paisley."

"Why would Paisley need a new bowl?" He

cocked his head to the side and thought about this. Understanding dawned a brief moment later. "NO!"

"Yes!" I insisted. "You'll be eating those new generic dry crunchies from Paisley's used dog bowl. And guess what else?"

He took a couple steps back and pressed himself against the wall. "Not my Evian."

"That's right. It's about time you developed a taste for tap water," I said with a shrug.

"You are an evil woman, Angela. A very evil woman."

I simply smiled and gave him a couple minutes to process everything.

Finally, he turned toward the line of kittens and lay down with his forelegs folded beneath him. "So if I agree to help, you'll agree to cancel any changes to my menu or dining service?"

"Correct. Plus the sooner we figure out what's going on with the kittens, the sooner we can find new homes for them—also the sooner we can get them out of your hair."

"I do like the sound of that," he conceded as one kitten yanked on his tail and another climbed onto his back. "But you should still know that I'm helping out of duress."

"Noted. Now let's get to work. I need your help talking to them."

He sighed, then yawned, then flopped onto his side.

The kittens pushed themselves against his belly and purred.

That was too much for Octo-Cat. He jumped back onto his feet and shouted, "Stop that! I am not your mama."

"Daddy," the kittens mewled merrily.

"I'm not that, either. I don't even know who you are. Maybe you can start by telling me that."

"Hungry," one of the other kittens said without properly pronouncing the *R,* so it came out more like *hungee.*

Octo-Cat looked to me. "Did you get that?"

I nodded, then translated for Charles, "They're hungry."

He pulled out his phone and began to browse the web in response.

"How old do you think they are?" I asked Octo-Cat.

"It's hard to say. A couple months, maybe."

Charles set his phone on top of the closed aquarium and lifted a kitten in one hand, then handed her to me. "That's about a pound, right?"

I nodded, unsure of it myself.

"Then we should be okay trying some soft cat food."

"Should I get some of Octo-Cat's?" I offered. It's not like we had anything else in the house that could work.

"Don't you dare!" he growled, startling the kittens.

"We need a special kind for kittens," Charles explained. "Could you text Nan back and ask her to get some from the store?"

"I could, but I didn't actually text her. That was a bluff."

Octo-Cat glowered at me, clearly not pleased with anything about our current situation.

"I'll head out then, if that's okay," Charles offered. "I'll be back as fast as I can." He placed a kiss on my forehead, then carefully let himself out of the room so that none of the felines could exit after him.

"Can I go now?" my cat asked me as the kittens continued to lick, nip, and bat at him.

"Sorry. I still need your help. Do you think the kittens will be willing to talk once they've been fed?"

"Maybe," he answered with an exhausted sigh.

"But little ones this age don't know very many words. Much more advanced than humans at this age, but still with nowhere near the intellect of a full-grown cat."

This was turning out to be quite the challenge. "Then what do we do?"

"I say we revisit the raccoon's idea to—"

"Don't finish that sentence if you know what's good for you."

"You're no fun," he groaned. "If you want to figure out what happened to them, you're going to have to mount an investigation, AKA you're going to have to do your job for a change."

Ouch.

But also... *touché.*

8

After Octo-Cat assured me he'd keep an eye on the little ones, I went to survey the scene of their abandonment. Other than a few bloody pawprints, the porch looked normal enough.

A faint pair of boot prints could just be made out under the fresh snowfall. I put my foot into one as a gauge for size. It was larger, but only just. Nothing about the style of the print gave away the wearer's gender, and I could find no other clues nearby.

Any tire tracks that may have been left behind had already mixed in with the ones Nan made when leaving for her fitness class. For all I knew the mysterious doorstep-dropper could have been on foot.

"I thought I smelled your unique aroma wafting through my treehouse." Pringle climbed up the porch railing and hopped down to stand beside me. I was pleased to see he'd left Carla at home. I was also quite offended by what he'd just said to me.

"How dare you say I stink!"

"I said you smelled," he corrected, wagging a finger at me. "Not *bad*, exactly. Not good, either, though."

I took a deep breath and forced myself to focus. If Pringle insisted on bothering me, maybe he could offer some assistance while he was here. "Did you see who brought the kittens?"

"Nope. I heard the car driving away but didn't get here in enough time to see anything."

Okay. So they were delivered by vehicle, which meant that someone had intentionally chosen my house for this very special delivery.

I could unpack that later. Right now I needed to use Pringle while I had him. "Usually you're so fast. How did you miss this?"

He sank to all fours and sighed. "I had to wait for a good place to pause my show."

"Survivor?"

"You know it. I'm on season twenty-seven, and it is definitely the most dramatic one yet."

Didn't he know they said that every season about every single reality show? Well, at least this addiction of his kept him from creating havoc for me 24/7.

"Uh-huh. Are you least learning valuable survival skills from all this binge-watching?"

He blew a raspberry. "Please. I watch it simply because it's so bad. I could teach these humans a thing or two or two hundred about wilderness survival. By the way, I sent in an application for next season, using your name and video."

It was already bad enough he snuck into my texts and social media. Now there was a video? Wait... what? "What video?" I boomed.

"Why, the one I took through your window when you weren't paying attention, of course." His answer came out flippantly, as if he saw nothing wrong with his actions at all. That made it worse, because it meant that things like this would happen again... and again.

And again.

I clenched my fists tight at my side but forced myself to keep calm. Recording private videos of me was definitely not okay. If he were a human, I would have called the police to come and get him.

Unfortunately, I still needed Pringle's help with the kittens. After that, I could rain down all kinds of punishment on him.

"Since you like spying and finding out secrets," I managed at last, still unable to look the raccoon in the eye, "maybe you can figure out where the kittens came from?"

"Where they came from?" he asked in that grating nasal voice of his, although perhaps I was coloring the situation red with the rage of his recent revelation. "Why does it matter?"

I balked. How could he not understand? "Because didn't you see all that blood?"

He shrugged off my concern. "So what? Blood happens. It's a fact of life."

"Not for humans, it doesn't. Blood usually means something has gone seriously wrong." How could he know so much about humans, yet still know so little? A lot of good all his reality TV viewing and covert spy operations were doing him.

"Yes, but you found *kittens,* didn't you? *Not humans,* so thus not a big deal."

"Still, it would really help put my mind at ease.

Can you just... I don't know... follow their scent or something?"

"Ex-squeeze me? Follow their scent? What do you think I am? Some kind of dog?"

I stared at him with my mouth open for a moment before answering.

Over the last year or so, I'd found there were two effective ways to deal with Pringle when I needed him to do something. The first was to give him something he wanted—treehouses, an adventure, a Nerf gun named Carla. The second, although harder to pull off, was much easier on the wallet. It was time to pull out this strategy and hope it did the trick.

It was time to employ reverse psychology.

"Aren't raccoons part of the dog family?" I knew that they weren't, but that was beside the point.

"Yeah, maybe the disgruntled cousin. Either way, we're not having Thanksgiving dinner together. Capiche?"

I frowned, all part of the act. "So you're saying raccoons can't smell as well as dogs? That's okay. I understand. Paisley will be home soon, so I can just—"

"Wash your mouth out with soap right now!

Raccoons are superior to dogs in every single way. I could sniff out the culprit if I wanted to."

"Yeah, but Paisley has a lot of experience. I bet she could trace the scent without even having to lower her nose to the ground."

The raccoon placed a hand on each hip. "I don't need experience to be the best. I was born that way. Now, you get out of my way!"

Satisfaction wrapped around me like a warm blanket as I watched Pringle scurry down the driveaway and out of sight. I hoped he'd be able to trace the source of the kittens, but even if he couldn't, at least he was out of the way for the next couple hours.

Meanwhile I had one more piece of evidence to process before calling in some outside help, and it was waiting for me in the upstairs bathroom.

To the box!

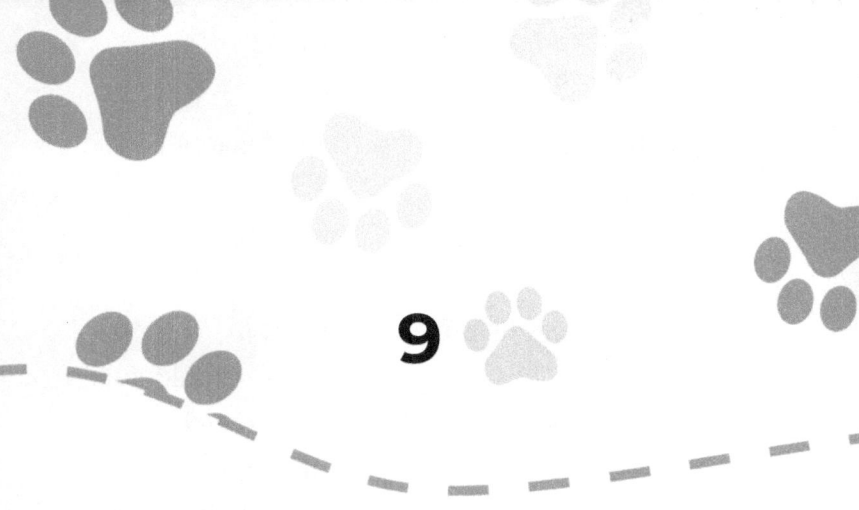

9

The box was not in good shape. Not only had it been soiled with bloody pawprints, but it had also been badly shredded around the top edges and the inside. Whoever had packed the kittens inside had decided to fold the top flaps inward rather than letting them hang down over the outside.

I pulled each of the flaps out to take a closer look. Sure enough, beneath all the stains and scratches, I spied a white shipping label. Would this give me the address of the person who'd dropped off the litter?

I grabbed a container of bleach wipes from under the bathroom sink and began to carefully dab at the label. By the time I was done, I had a partial address:

1 8 ir S

Gle le, E

Well, that was helpful.

I could tell that the second line should read Glendale, Maine, but the first was so scratched up I found it impossible to read more than two numbers and three letters. None of which helped my tired brain.

Maybe Charles or Nan would have some idea. I'd be sure to ask them when they returned home.

For now, I was all out of clues—and Octo-Cat was probably all out of patience. I took a snapshot of the address label for safekeeping and then returned to the cat room.

I'd left the cats alone for fifteen minutes at most, but the scene that greeted me upon my return felt lightyears apart from the one I'd left behind.

Octo-Cat had lined up the kittens in a straight row right in front of the fish tank. He now walked back and forth, holding his tail high and erect as he spoke. "To be a cat, you have to be strong, brave, and—above all—well-groomed. Do you understand me?"

"Daddy! Yes, Daddy!" the kittens shouted in

unison. Their high-pitched baby voices made this scene even more absurd than the fact they were cats.

Octo-Cat did an about-face, unable to hide the smug grin on his face even as he caught sight of me.

"What are you doing?" I asked cautiously, curious but also not wanting an earful.

"Training up the new recruits," he barked—or at least made a canine-like noise, one I'd never heard him utter before.

"Daddy! Yes, Daddy!" the kittens responded in kind.

While I was glad he'd changed his stance on spending time with the youngsters, I was also now very worried. "Training them to do what exactly?"

"To be cats, of course. It's a very important and very demanding job." My cat grinned a jokeresque grin, which would have frightened me were it not so comical.

I choked down a laugh. "I'm sure it is. How much do they even understand?"

"While it's true their vocabulary is limited, it's never too early to begin training. Also I'm more than happy to lead by example. Watch and learn." He turned back to his recruits and plopped his rear down before them, then lifted one paw to his forehead in salute and waited for the kittens to respond in kind.

"Are you ready for your next lesson?" he shouted.

"Daddy! Yes, Daddy!" they shouted.

Well, it seemed Nan and Paisley weren't the only ones to go to boot camp today. There was entirely too much shouting going on.

"I call this one operative 037. Observe." Octo-Cat came flying in my direction, suddenly pulling to a stop just before smashing headfirst into my legs.

I winced, expecting some kind of attack, but all he did was rub his head lovingly against me. A loud purr rumbled in his throat as he glanced back toward the line of kittens.

Aww, this was nice. He was teaching the babies how to be little love balls. I didn't know he had it in him.

"Now you give it a try, cadets!" he shouted again, jarring my nerves.

The kittens trotted over and rubbed their heads and bodies against my feet and ankles, just as their instructor had done.

"Well done. Well done, indeed." Octo-Cat took a brief moment to dote on them, then shifted back into business mode. "From here we'll move straight into operative 038."

Before I could ask what was next, Octo-Cat sank his front claws into my leg and climbed from the floor to my shoulder, using me as his ladder.

"Ahhhh!" I cried, but it did nothing to stop all five kittens from following suit. "I don't like this!"

Octo-Cat ignored me as he jumped down onto the floor. "All right. Now disengage."

"Daddy! Yes, Daddy!" One brave kitten leaped to the ground, but the others went back the way they'd come—down my poor, pained body.

"Why would you teach them that?" I moaned as I pushed myself flat against the closed door.

Octo-Cat studied his paw rather than looking at me. "We cats have to use any resources at our disposal."

Ouch. Way to add insult to injury. "Is that all I am to you? *A resource?*"

"It's not *all* you are, but it is part of it. Trust me, you'll be glad I've trained them up. Just wait and see."

"They aren't staying," I muttered as several pinpoints on my body pulsed with pain. Now I was even more determined to see the kittens safely off than Octo-Cat had been earlier that afternoon.

Had he planned it this way? The evil genius.

"Listen," I continued, still pressed firmly against the door and eyeing my cat warily. "You've done a great job looking after them. Why don't you take a little break?"

He scoffed and took a step closer. "And leave their education to you? I think not."

Crud. Well, it was worth a try. If he insisted on turning the kittens into some kind of deranged domestic soldiers, I could at least make sure I wasn't around for the next operative. The kittens had already lined back up and were awaiting further instruction when I crept out of the room and headed back downstairs.

I still couldn't believe how quickly Octo-Cat had changed his tune about our litter of foundlings. We needed to find them homes and fast, before my ever-scheming cat used them to execute total world domination.

What? I wouldn't put it past him.

Both Charles and Pringle would be back soon. Until then I would wait safely on the porch and scroll through my social media feeds to pass time.

It didn't take long for someone to return, and that someone was Nan. She and Paisley looked wicked worn out, which was rare for them.

"How was class?" I asked as the two of them crept slowly up the porch steps.

"Painful." Nan winced with each movement. "Now what are you doing out here?"

"Hiding from the cats," I explained, although it embarrassed me somewhat.

My grandmother paused and shot me a worried look. *"Cats?* As in plural? Am I going senile already? I could have sworn we just had the one."

I nodded. "It's a long story. Come upstairs, and I'll show you."

Nan shook her head slowly. "I'm not sure I'm ready to tackle the big stairs just yet. It may take me a few hours. At least until these pulsing fireworks stop going off in my quads."

"She did, like, a million squats," the equally exhausted Chihuahua informed me. "But not once did she go potty."

I chuckled at this. "Did you do squats, too?"

Paisley wagged her tail at my attention. "Nope. There was a big dog there, and we wrestled while the humans busted their booties."

"Did you at least win?"

"Oh, yeah," she barked happily. "That will teach that silly old Great Dane to underestimate me!"

Ha! Our sweet Paisley, always full of surprises.

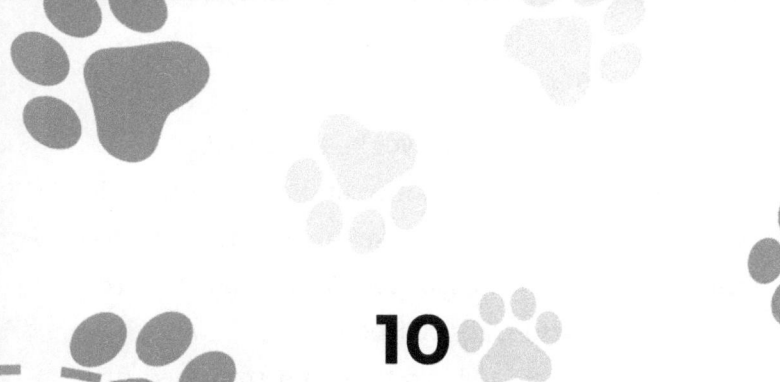

10

Once inside, I helped Nan get settled on the couch. And with every gasp and groan that escaped her mouth, I thanked my lucky stars there hadn't been an open spot for me in her new fitness class.

"You wait here," I told her after fluffing a pillow behind her back. "I'll go get the kittens."

Paisley followed me up the stairs, whining slightly as she went.

I turned to look back at her, but she just kept climbing like a champ. "I thought you were tired, too?"

Her ears perked up. "I am, but I still want to go with you, Mommy. I missed you while Nan and I were away."

Why couldn't my cat ever be this nice?

Even though she was nice and even though she was tired, I still couldn't take any chances when it came to the kittens. I scooped Paisley into my arms and entered Octo-Cat's bedroom.

Paisley let out a sharp bark and squirmed furiously in my arms. "Oh, my! Puppies! Cat puppies!"

"Don't be so insulting." Octo-Cat sniffed derisively. "These are kittens. Not *cat puppies,* you simpleton."

Paisley didn't so much as whimper at the insult. She was far too excited to care. "Please set me down, Mommy!" she begged. "I want to go say hi!"

The moment I did, she bounded over to the line of kitty cadets and squealed happily as she licked the insides of each young feline's ears.

They giggled and fell to their sides.

"Can't you see I'm leading a class here?" Octo-Cat seethed, his tail twitching aggressively.

"Yes. And your class is about to take a field trip. Nan wants to meet them."

"Then have her come up here? It's best we don't disturb their environment. Otherwise it could undo all their training."

If only. With any luck they'd forget operative 038 forever.

I sucked air through my teeth and shook my head. "No can do, Mr. Kitty. Nan is stuck downstairs, so we're taking the babies to her."

"How many times have I told you not to call me that?" Octo-Cat sighed heavily as the two of us watched Paisley cuddle and lick the mass of kittens. It's official; they're ruined now.

"Mommy?" one of the kitties asked the others as she cuddled up to the doting Chihuahua.

"Mommy!" the rest cheered in response.

Octo-Cat gasped.

I chuckled.

Paisley trotted over to us with the kittens ambling behind. "Mommy," she addressed me, "the cat puppies are calling for you."

I bent down to scratch between her ears. "Actually, I think they're calling for *you*. They've decided you're their mommy."

"Me? A mommy? Oh my love!" Paisley's dark eyes welled with tears. In just a few more weeks, the kittens would probably all be larger than Paisley, but she would now forever be their mother—I had no doubt about that.

"Mommy," the kittens cooed, and then turning to Octo-Cat, "Daddy!"

"Octavius," Paisley warbled, still crying tears of joy. "We have puppies together. Does that mean we should get married?"

"I'm ready to go now, Angela," Octo-Cat informed me, turning to face the door, his voice devoid of any emotion—the poor guy had clearly had his fill of insanity for one day.

"Paisley, can you watch them for a minute? I'll be right back."

"Yes, Mommy." She returned to her litter and started a game of chase. She'd gone from zero to sixty mighty fast upon meeting the kitties.

"Hey, now you're Grand-Mommy!" she pointed out just as I was shutting the door behind Octo-Cat.

Oh, great. I wasn't ready to marry and have my own kids, but somehow I'd become a grandma anyway. *Wonderful.*

Brushing that thought aside, I went to retrieve the cat carrier from storage. I needed some way to get the kittens downstairs, and it just didn't feel right putting them back in that bloody, battered box.

Paisley spoke calmly to her litter as I loaded them into the carrier, making the task a piece of cake.

Once downstairs, I set the carrier beside Nan on the couch and opened the wire mesh door.

"This is Nan. She's *Great Nan* to you," the proud doggie mother informed them. "Be careful not to fall or jump off the couch. We Chihuahuas are a fragile breed."

Just as I was wondering whether Paisley understood that these were not her actual babies, Nan caught sight of the kittens for the first time and gasped with delight.

"Where did you come from?" she squealed in the high-pitched voice she normally reserved only for Paisley.

I caught Nan up on the particulars while she petted and cuddled the babies.

"How horrible! What kind of monster would abandon such sweet babies?" she asked once I'd finished.

I shook my head, still at a loss. "I'm less concerned with why someone would leave them here than with where the blood came from."

"Blood?" Paisley barked. "Are my cat puppies hurt? We need to go to the vet right now!"

Not only was the little dog proving to be quite the helicopter parent, but she also had a really good idea. I would have chastised myself for not thinking of it earlier, but we'd only found them very recently and have been very busy trying to figure out where they came from, get them food, and make sure they stayed out of trouble.

"We should go to the vet," I agreed with a nod. "They don't seem hurt, but it's better to know for sure."

"Let's go now. I need to make sure my puppies are okay!" Paisley whined and gave out another round of licks. For whatever reason, the Chihuahua seemed to think that inner-ear kisses could solve anything. If I wasn't careful, she'd sneak up on me and push her warm, wet tongue into my ear, too.

Luckily, Charles pulled into the drive just then, causing Paisley to temporarily forget her panic and instead start barking in excitement.

The kittens mewled their best attempts at a bark, and I broke apart in laughter. It seemed Paisley wasn't the only one confused about what species our litter belonged to.

"I'm back," Charles sang as he passed through the foyer and joined us in the living room. "Did you miss me?"

I smiled in relief. "You have no idea how much."

He really didn't. Even though less than an hour had passed, a record-breaking amount of activity had occurred.

Charles set the bag from the pet store on the table and pulled out a pair of stainless-steel bowls. Next he took out the canned cat food and pulled the tabs to open them.

The kittens definitely recognized the smell as being something to eat.

"Hungry!" they cried in their cutesy baby voices, stumbling toward the edge of the couch.

Paisley managed to catch one by the scruff of its neck before it toppled over the edge. "Careful, my darling dear."

Charles, Nan, and I placed the kittens on the floor with the two bowls of food and watched them gobble it down.

"Should I open up another can?" he asked me with a questioning glance.

"Better not. They still have tiny bellies, and I don't want them to get sick. Especially since we're going to the vet after this."

"I'm not going!" Octo-Cat called from the other room.

"You're not invited!" I shouted back. Now that Paisley had graciously taken responsibility for the litter, we didn't need drill instructor Octavius's help any longer.

Let's just hope the poor doggie foster mom didn't become too attached. I'd hate to see her heart break when we sent them off to their forever homes.

11

And off to the veterinarian's clinic we went.
Charles called ahead to let them
know we were stopping by without an
appointment, but that the adorable kittens would
surely make it worth their while.

The three of us must have made quite the spec-
tacle as we marched into the animal hospital,
holding the mewing crate high as their Chihuahua
mother ran at our sides yapping a constant stream
of encouragement.

"Don't worry, my cat puppies. You're not sick.
The doctor's just going to make sure you stay that
way. It's all part of growing up. You will be brave for
Mommy, won't you?"

"Mommy! Yes, Mommy!" Well, it seemed not all of Octo-Cat's training had been forgotten.

"Let me guess," the receptionist said as she rose to her feet and peeked into the cat carrier. "You must be the Russo party."

"That's us," I confirmed with a nod, even though I was the only one whose last name was actually Russo.

"Come with me. Dr. Lowe is just finishing up with another patient. She should be with you short-ly." She smiled and motioned for us to follow, swinging her hips the whole way.

We obediently followed her into exam room two.

"Good luck!" the receptionist called, closing us inside.

Charles remained standing so that Nan and I could take the two chairs. "Did you see that her scrubs had pawprints and bones on them? That is so neat. I wish lawyers got more interesting clothing options, but everyone in the courtroom would look at me like I was crazy if I came wearing a suit with a gavel or the scales of justice patterned all over it."

"You should do it anyway," Nan offered with a wink. After all, she was the queen of outrageous costumes. She'd wear just about anything, just so long as it was the right shade of pink.

I laughed uncomfortably. At least Christmas had already passed, or else Nan might be gifting my boyfriend with a new hot pink lawyer suit. *Cringe.*

As promised, a few minutes later, Dr. Britt Lowe entered the room, clipboard in hand. She was the youngest of all the veterinarians in the office and the one who most regularly saw our pets. She widened her eyes and puckered her lips as she took us in. "I hear you have kittens."

"Not intentionally," I was quick to clarify, though I'm not sure why. "They were left on our doorstep this morning."

She glanced down at her chart. "I have a note here that they were covered in blood?"

"Well, not covered," Charles explained. "But they had it on their paws and a little in their fur as well. We had to give them a bath."

"That must have been fun," the vet said with a chuckle. "Let's take them out and have a look. One at a time, if you don't mind."

"Okay, children," Paisley barked. "Be good for the doctor. No biting or growling."

Dr. Lowe bent down and gave the dog a pat. "Oh, hello. I didn't see you there, Paisley."

"She's become quite attached to the litter," I said with a frown. Every single minute that passed before rehoming the kittens would only add to Paisley's eventual heartbreak.

"I bet your cat is none too pleased," Dr. Lowe said with another chuckle.

"You would definitely win that bet." Yes, even among other cat lovers, my cat had a reputation for being a diva. He couldn't help that he was raised in excessive luxury for his first several years, but still.

Charles handed our vet the first of the kittens.

"Hello, there, you cutie pie," she cooed. "This is why I love my job."

A huge grin stretched across her face as she examined the patient. "Girl. About seven or eight weeks. Most likely a Maine Coon or Maine Coon mix."

She placed a stethoscope against the kitten's tiny chest. "Heartbeat is good, and from what I can see, she has no injuries."

"So the blood wasn't hers?" Nan asked, her hands clasped against her chest.

"No, but I still have four others to examine."

I took the first kitten back, and Charles handed Dr. Lowe the second. This one was also deemed fit as a fiddle.

One by one, the doctor declared each baby—three girls and two boys—healthy and without injury.

"So then where did the blood come from?" Charles wanted to know.

Dr. Lowe shook her head. "Sorry, but I couldn't say."

"Are there many litters abandoned on people's doorsteps around Glendale?" I pressed. I was glad the kittens passed their health check but felt uncomfortable leaving without any answers as to their origin.

"This would be the first I've come across it," she responded, which didn't mean much given how short a time she'd been working here. "Do you think it was a random drive-by or that someone meant to leave these kittens with you specifically?"

Charles answered for me. "That's what we're trying to figure out."

"And not having much luck, unfortunately," I added with a heavy sigh.

"Well, the important thing is that they're safe now that they're with you. If you need help finding them homes, we could put a flyer up in the office," she suggested while jotting a note on her chart. "No charge for today's visit. Good luck!"

Having been dismissed, we settled the kittens back in their carrier. I was still so confused by their sudden appearance. Could someone be sending me a threat? Is that why they'd been covered in blood? It may seem farfetched, but I'd had my life threatened before—so why not now? Why not with this?

"What should we do now?" I asked Charles.

But it was Nan who answered. "For whatever reason, these kittens found us. I say we provide them with a loving home and stop worrying about the rest."

"Yes! Yes! Let's do that!" Paisley yipped with excitement, then ran fast, tight circles around the office. Zoomies.

"Nan," I growled. "These are things we should discuss *in private.*"

She crimsoned under the scrutiny of my gaze but didn't apologize for making the suggestion.

"Do you want to keep one?" I asked Charles.

"Jacques and Jillianne would never forgive me if I brought another animal home. You know that." He was right. His two hairless cats weren't exactly hospitable. They also spoke only in rhymes and riddles, which would, no doubt, drive any kitty we sent to live with them batty.

Thankfully, Nan and Paisley both remained

quiet as we made our way out of the clinic. Was I a bad person for not wanting to add an army of cats into my daily life? I mean, who knew what kind of damage Octo-Cat could do to their psyches with the opportunity to raise them up from this young age? My side still hurt from where Octavius and all five kitties had climbed up my leg and torso. No, I definitely couldn't handle this kind of havoc every single day.

Another thought popped into my mind and scared the living daylights out of me. *What if the kittens wanted to help with the P.I. business? Dealing with one cat already took a great deal of both patience and delicacy, but six?*

No, thank you. I'd sooner work as an underappreciated paralegal for the rest of my days.

"We're not keeping them," I sputtered a couple minutes later, my mind more than made up. "But we will make sure each of them finds the perfect home."

Nan crossed her arms over her chest and pouted while Charles nodded his agreement. "We'll find them great homes," he said, lacing his fingers through mine.

I looked to Paisley who lay dejectedly on my lap. "I guess all puppies have to grow up some day.

I just didn't know it would come this soon for mine."

I had to bite my tongue to keep from reminding her that she'd only known her "puppies" for less than an hour.

The clock was ticking fast. Now I needed to protect both the kittens and their dog mom. Nothing else mattered until we could find a way to give everyone a happy ending.

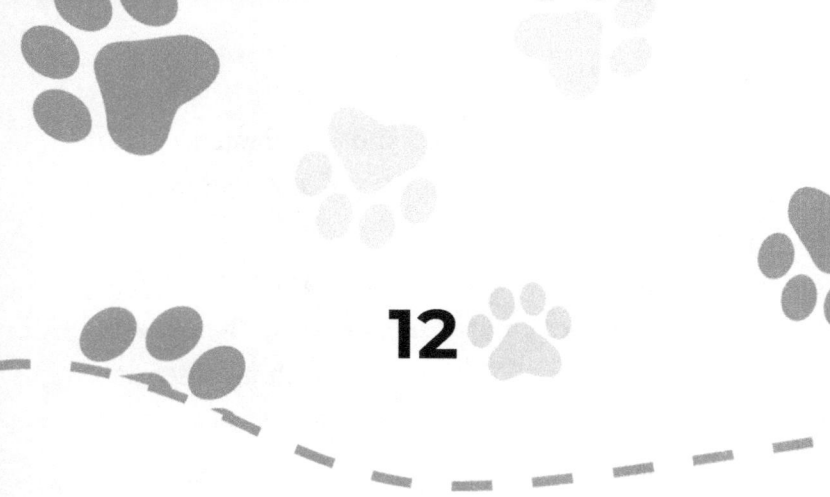

12

Once we'd made it home again, Paisley tended to the kittens in the living room while Nan prepared lunch for the humans.

Charles and I ventured up to my work library to work on posting an ad for the kittens online and to design a flyer for the vet's office. Despite Pringle's earnest advice, we were offering them free to a good home—provided the would-be owner could provide a great veterinarian reference.

"I'm sorry our big day together got ruined," I told Charles while navigating the same free graphics program I'd used to create a simplistic logo for the Pet Whisperer P.I. website.

Charles moved behind me and rubbed my

shoulders while I worked and we chatted. "What are you talking about? This is great. A real memory in the making."

"I guess it's better than watching TV," I conceded, although I wouldn't pass up the opportunity to cuddle and relax with my dashing other half. In truth, we never took it easy, such was the nature of our crazy lives.

A rapping at the big bay window broke my concentration. Our not-so-friendly neighborhood raccoon stood on the ledge, waiting to be let in. This happened somewhat frequently these days and was why I no longer kept a screen in the window.

"What's up?" I asked after cranking it open.

"What's... up?" Pringle asked, gasping for breath between the two words. "That all... you got? After I... tracked those... annoying little... furballs for... you?"

Oh, yes! In all the fuss, I'd almost forgotten that I'd sent him on a fact-finding/ raccoon-distracting mission. "Welcome back. What have you got for me?"

He hopped down and pressed a hand against the wall for support. "First refreshments... Then I'll spill."

"Be right back," I told Charles.

"What?" he asked, taken aback. "Don't leave me alone with that thing!"

"With this *thing?*" Pringle raged. "With this thing? I'll have you know that I'm the most pedigreed—" Suddenly his words gave way and he moved one furry hand to clutch his chest. "I mean... Please... Need food."

"Nice try. I don't like lying," I scolded, returning to my desk chair and spinning in it to face him. "I'll feed you, but you'll talk first."

Knowing the act was up, Pringle straightened his posture and cracked his neck to either side. "Fine."

I waited for him to comb at his fur with his fingers as he gathered his bearings.

Finally he began. "I ran for miles but got nowhere with the case."

"Did you even try?" I asked with indignation. He'd been gone for so long, I'd let myself hope he'd found something. *No dice.*

"You insult me," he hissed and bared his teeth. "Of course I tried. I asked every animal I came across, but nobody knew nothing about no orphaned kittens."

"When this is all over and done, we need to

work on your grammar," I muttered without thinking.

Pringle dropped to all fours and raised his back, making his body appear much larger than its usual size. "Really? I spend all morning doing your dirty work, and this is the thanks I get? I'm leaving."

"Wait. I'm sorry. Let me get you some food first. Fancy Feast?" Even though Octo-Cat had switched to a new brand of cat food called Delectable Delights to support his girlfriend's modeling career, I still had to buy Fancy Feast to satisfy the raccoon's frequent cravings.

"Yes, and some steak, please," he added while licking his chops.

"How much is *some* steak?"

"How much you got?"

"I'll get it," Charles offered. As he passed me, he leaned close and whispered, "That way you can't be held accountable if I get it wrong."

"I heard that," Pringle complained to me once Charles had left the room. "And now you owe me double. Quality or quantity, it's your choice, but I wouldn't turn my nose up at some prime rib served medium rare. You never buy me the good cuts of steak."

I never bought the good cuts for myself, either. And weren't raccoons supposed to feed themselves?

Nope. I wasn't falling for his sob story.

"Sorry. I don't think so. Not after you've invaded my privacy left and right."

"I don't get humans' obsession with *privacy.*" He made air quotes around this last word. "It's not like you give any to us."

I refused to let him get away with that one. "What are you talking about? I never bother you. It's always the other way around."

"So now I'm a bother?"

"That's not what I meant. It's just—"

"Just what?" He widened his eyes in challenge while awaiting my response.

Reasoning with him never got me very far, and I was too busy with everything else to bother trying now. "Forget it," I said with a deep sigh.

"Yeah, like I said, you owe me, but don't worry. I already know exactly what I want, and it won't cost you much at all."

Oh, joy. Maybe if I didn't respond, he would keep quiet until Charles returned with the raccoon's ill-gotten gains.

"I love my Carla, but I think I'm ready to handle

two of her kind," he explained while he mimed taking aim at me with the gun. Thank goodness I knew Carla was what he had named his Nerf weapon, otherwise I'd be seriously offended for all womankind—human, raccoon, or otherwise.

"I'm not getting you another Nerf gun," I said firmly. If I showed any signs of weakness, he'd pounce.

"It's okay if it's not name brand. I ain't picky."

"Great."

"You can deliver it to my left treehouse by sundown." And didn't that say it all? The fact he had to specify *which* treehouse he wanted to receive the hypothetical delivery.

"I'm not doing anything until we figure out the deal with these kittens," I said, more than fed up with his demands. "And if you'll recall, you didn't actually even help."

"Hey, that's not my fault! I tried!" he squeaked. Finally he'd begun to lose his cool, which meant he was also losing his leverage.

"Okay, who's ready for some lunch?" Charles sang as he rejoined us. He'd brought up two plates with grilled gruyere and tomato sandwiches and a grocery bag stuffed full of assorted junk food.

"Nan wanted us to eat up here so she could have some alone time with the kittens," he said in response to my unspoken question.

"And this, my man, is for you." He handed the shopping bag to Pringle, who eagerly accepted it.

"Door, please," he told me without so much as a backward glance my way.

I had no desire to keep him around, so I opened the door and watched him clamber down the stairs. The pet door was still closed, so I had to follow him down to assist.

"I'm starved," I said upon returning.

Charles settled into the window seat and waited for me to join him.

I accepted the plate he handed to me and took a giant bite of my sandwich after mumbling a quick thanks—so warm, so gooey. I shrugged and took another bite.

We scarfed down our sandwiches in much the same way the kittens had inhaled their meal earlier.

"Any idea why Nan would need some alone time with the kittens?" Charles wiped at his mouth with a napkin. "You don't think she's going to pull something to try to make you keep them? Do you?"

I jumped to my feet and cried, "Well, I didn't before! C'mon, we've got to hurry!"

I tugged Charles's hand, pulling him into the hall and down the stairs. If we were fast, we could still stop her from whatever it was she planned to pull.

Oh, that nan of mine!

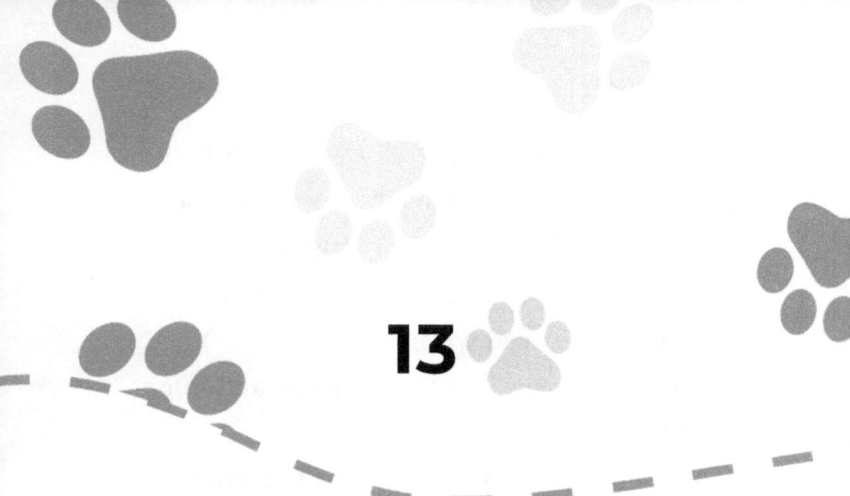

13

Sure enough, the only thing we found downstairs was a smug Octo-Cat sitting on the coffee table and quite obviously waiting for us.

"Missing something?" he asked with a cruel chuckle as a Cheshire grin swept across his face.

Well, that confirmed it. Nan had hit the road and taken the kittens along with her. "How long has she been gone?" I asked the still gloating cat.

"She left the very minute UpChuck headed upstairs with the food." He yawned and stretched before settling back into a seated position. "By the way, nobody offered to feed me."

Oh, boy. I could already tell this would take a

while. Nan could make it all the way to Florida in the time it took me to convince my cat to help.

"You never have lunch," I reminded him gently, all the while praying my instincts about this encounter were dead wrong.

"You only eat in the morning and night," I added pathetically.

"It's still nice to be asked. Especially since I know you promised the raccoon steak."

"I definitely never promised anything."

"Well, it seems we've reached an impasse then." He turned around so that his back was to me. I could just imagine him laughing at my gullibility, but I didn't have any time to spare if I wanted to protect Paisley's feelings and discover where Nan had taken the kittens—and I definitely wanted to do both of those things ASAP.

"Do you know where she went?" I asked in a shaky whisper.

He flicked his tail twice and then slowly shifted back my way. "Maybe," came his curt reply.

Maybe wasn't yes, but it also wasn't no. I'd have to play his little game, whether I liked it or not. I couldn't hold back my sigh as I asked, "All right, what's it going to take? A can of food?"

"*Pffffshaw.* It'll take a lot more than that." Octo-

Cat's eyes glowed as he licked at his chops. "Like steak, for starters."

"Do you actually like steak? You've never even tried it." Although I'd only just eaten, now my stomach rumbled, too.

"No, I haven't. And honestly that's the whole problem. You just don't consider me and my needs as much as you should."

I held my breath to keep from screaming. My whole life revolved around my crabby tabby and his wants and needs.

He sniffed and turned his nose up at me. "I will require at least nine steaks, one for each of the lives I was born with."

I sighed and nodded along with his lengthy list of demands. The sooner we got this over with, the sooner he might actually help me.

"I will also need a lobster roll from Little Dog Diner."

He paused to take a breath, and I jumped in with another objection. "But Little Dog Diner is all the way over in Misty Harbor."

"I know where it is. I also know they make the best lobster rolls in all of the bay, so you're going."

I gritted my teeth and clenched my fists. "Fine. Anything else?"

"Yes. I saved the best for last." His smile laced a knot of dread into my heart. Heaven help me.

"You see," he continued, unaware of how anxious I'd become during our very one-sided conversation. "As much as I enjoy spending time with Pringle *on occasion,* he's been rather insufferable lately."

"Let me guess. Carla." This, we actually agreed on. Maybe we could join forces to teach that raccoon a lesson.

Octo-Cat made a clicking noise and waved a paw my way. "Bingo."

"So what? You want a Nerf gun, too?" I asked with a chuckle.

"Oh, Angela. Haven't you noticed that I don't have any opposable thumbs? Really, I thought you were more observant than that. I need a specialized weapon that doesn't discriminate against those of us without thumbs."

I sighed. Maybe we weren't on the same side, after all. "Such as?" I asked politely.

My cat's eyes locked on mine, trapping me within his gaze. "I was thinking a battle axe."

"Are you kidding me?" I sputtered in disbelief. "There's no way I'm getting you a battle axe. You'd chop my foot off the first time I forgot to feed you."

"Maybe that's a sign you shouldn't forget to feed me."

He let out a sinister laugh as phantom pain smarted in my ankle. There would definitely be no battle axe.

"I do my best. You know that. I'm not getting you a battle axe, though. So try again."

He cleared his throat and tried again. "A sword."

I shook my head.

"Mace."

"Like pepper spray?" I asked. "I guess that's not so bad. I can—"

"No, Angela. Not like pepper spray. Like a big spiky ball on the end of a chain."

"Remind me again why you need all this heavy-duty medieval weaponry?" I managed to choke out. This wasn't the first time I'd been afraid of my cat, but it was the worst. Talk about an unstable genius.

"To defend myself," he answered as if this all made perfect sense to him.

"Against foam darts?"

Octo-Cat smiled and nodded. "Precisely."

"I could get you a foam sword," I offered with a sad shrug. "Or maybe a toy lightsaber. That would be fun. Um, wouldn't it?"

He rose to his feet and paced the length of the

coffee table. "Angela, really! Real problems require real solutions, not a cheap childproof stand-in."

Rather than pointing out that Pringle's weapon was also a toy, I remained quiet. It seemed every time I spoke, the rabbit hole I'd fallen down grew deeper and deeper.

The wheels in Octo-Cat's brain, however, continued to crank. He started and stopped several times before finally saying something that made sense. "You seem to be biased against medieval weapons. How about we turn to the martial arts instead?"

Yes, martial arts. He'd only have as much power as he held within his own paws. That wasn't so scary. It could actually work.

I nodded vigorously to show him how much I liked that idea. "I'm sure we could sneak you into a dojo so you can learn some self-defense moves."

"That's not what I meant, and I'm guessing you know that. I don't want to dirty my paws on that feral beast. I need a weapon to do it for me, so how about nunchucks?"

"Nunchucks?" I squeaked.

"Yes, I can hold one end in my mouth and swing the other to hit Pringle with," he explained matter-of-factly.

"Do you promise not to use them on me?"

He glanced toward Charles.

"Or Charles!" I added.

My cat shook his head as if his answer pained him. "Sadly, I can't promise that, but I can promise I'll cancel my plans to ransack your bedroom if you agree."

Wonderful, another bribe.

"Okay, fine. I'll get you nunchucks if it's so important to you. Now, tell me, what do you know about Nan's whereabouts?"

Octo-Cat gave me a Cheshire grin and hopped down from the coffee table. "I don't know where she went, but I do know how you can find her. If you'll just follow me please."

I waved for Charles to come with us, too.

"Why were you and your cat just discussing all those weapons?" he wanted to know.

"Trust me, it's not that unusual for us." This was sad because it was true.

"Talking animals are weird." Charles laughed, but I couldn't bring myself to—the image of my crazy cat swinging a battle axe was still too fresh in my mind.

14

Octo-Cat led us to the backyard where Pringle sat holed up in one of his tree-houses watching *Survivor* with the volume turned up to its max.

"Pringle. I brought you a client!" Octo-Cat shouted from the base of the tree.

"We are not clients," I hissed at the tabby. "I'm more like his landlord."

A few moments later, the TV clicked off and Pringle stuck his masked face out the window. "Have they brought payment?" he asked, ignoring me and Charles entirely.

"No, but they're good for it." Octo-Cat nudged me forward with his paw.

"Excellent," the raccoon chittered and climbed

down with surprising speed to join us on the lawn. He put on a phony grin and reached forward to offer his hand. "Pringle Whisperer, P.I., here. How can I help you today?"

I declined to shake it and instead nodded toward Octo-Cat. "I already paid him to help. I'm not paying you, too."

"That was my finder's fee," the cat corrected. "Pringle Whisperer, P.I., requires his payments to be arranged separately."

I threw my hands up in the air. How did we ever get anything done around here? "Can we stop wasting time, already? And can't either of you ever do anything just to be nice for a change?"

Octo-Cat and Pringle laughed for a solid five minutes at that one.

"What's going on?" Charles asked me, leaning close so I could hear him over the two guffawing animals.

"He wants another bribe, or he won't help us."

"Oh, no problem. I'll take care of it." Charles took out his wallet and began thumbing through a stack of folded dollar bills. "How much does he need?"

I knew my boyfriend made good money as the senior partner for the region's busiest law firm, but it surprised me when he didn't even hesitate to offer a giant wad of cash to our dear raccoon racketeer.

Pringle, however, refused to accept his generous payment. "Sorry, bro. Human money's no good here."

"But you can use it to buy things," I pointed out.

He made a face. "That's too hard. I'd rather not have to worry about the math. Besides, I've never once found a human shop owner willing to sell me what I needed. That's speciesism, I tell you, and I'm not okay with it."

"Okay, what do you want then?" And why had my entire day turned into agreeing to give everyone whatever they asked for? With the likes of Pringle and Octo-Cat around, this was a very dangerous proposition, indeed.

"Besides the steak you've already promised me and the new friend for Carla, I'll need—"

"I'm getting nine steaks," Octo-Cat stopped grooming his coat to brag.

"Cool, cool. Make it nine for me, too," Pringle confirmed.

"And a lobster roll," my cat betrayed me once more.

"Sure. I'll also take that." The raccoon rubbed

his hands together in anticipation of all the tasty things coming his way.

"Stop helping!" I shouted at my cat.

Pringle chittered blissfully. "This is awesome. We should work together more often, my fine feline friend." He stuck out his hand, and Octo-Cat gave him a high paw.

It was official. My life was over. Dealing with the two of them separately was already hard enough. Them joining forces fell into nightmare territory.

"I'll also require a new plasma TV," Pringle added as if it were one last small negotiation and not a gigantic expense.

"I'm out of here!" I stomped away, resigning myself to never finding Nan, Paisley, or the kittens again. There was negotiation and then there was extortion. I would have no part of that.

Pringle scurried in front of me and threw his hands up. "No, wait! It doesn't have to be plasma, but I do need a television. I really do."

"You already have one." I crossed my arms and gave him the stink eye. I may have been a softie, but I was no fool. I'd already bought him his own TV not too long ago.

"What's he asking for?" Charles wanted to know.

"A TV," I spat, still reeling from the audacious request.

"Doesn't he already have one?"

See, even Charles knew.

The raccoon put his hands together and begged. "Please. I wouldn't ask if I didn't desperately need it." He was an incredible actor, but he couldn't summon tears on demand.

I wasn't buying it. "Why the desperation?"

He hung his head and sniffed. "Because my TV-less treehouse is jealous of my TV-full treehouse."

I rolled my eyes at that. "Sorry, no. Treehouses don't have feelings."

"Fine, fine, fine, fine, fine! I'd like to use my houses more equally but don't want to spend time away from my show while I do it."

"That means you *don't* need two treehouses, not that you *do* need two TVs," I explained just as a headache swarmed by brain.

Charles placed a gentle hand on my shoulder. "I know you're worried about the kittens. Let's just get to them, okay? I'll pick up a TV for him later this week."

Pringle raised his index finger in objection. "Actually, I need it—"

"Later this week," I interrupted with the best scowl I could muster. "Take it or leave it."

The raccoon's whole demeanor softened. "You drive a tough bargain, Angie Russo, but sold! Now how can I help?"

"I need to know where Nan went with Paisley and the kittens."

"I don't know where they went, but I can find out."

"How long will that take?"

"I'll do it right now. Wait there." He climbed back into his treehouse and returned with iPad in hand. That was another excessive luxury we'd given him. True, it was Octo-Cat's old iPad, but why did either of them need their own personal tablet?

Sticking his tongue out while he worked, Pringle tapped the iPad several times, cycling through a number of apps until he found the one he wanted. He turned it toward me, revealing a flashing yellow dot moving along a map. "There. She's on the highway. Good?"

It was good, but it was also suspicious. "How did you do that?"

"I've got high-tech trackers on all of you. If one

of you goes somewhere, I can trace your phones to see where it is." He puffed with obvious pride. "I actually have you to thank for giving me the idea and for letting me use your credit card to purchase the licensing I needed."

Once again, my privacy had been unforgivably violated by this rascally raccoon. I didn't know he'd used my credit card for this. Had he used it for other things, too? I clearly needed to keep a better eye on my expenses. I also needed to report my card stolen and to invest in a small safe. I could keep my wallet and electronics locked inside every night to curtail Pringle's all too pervasive snooping.

Ugh. This was seriously getting out of hand.

15

We took a few minutes to set up a family plan on our devices. Once we had it in place, I was able to use Pringle's sneaky app to track Nan's location while Charles and I drove after her in pursuit.

"Stay here and call me on FaceTime if she comes back before we do," I instructed Octo-Cat, who agreed without too much pressure. Hmm. Maybe he felt guilty about driving up Pringle's payment by sharing what I'd agreed to give him—or maybe he just wanted to avoid the car trip.

Charles placed my phone into the clip on his dashboard and studied the map for a moment before starting up his engine. "She's got close to a half-hour lead on us, and she's still driving. "Wherever she went, it's pretty far."

I leaned closer to the dash to study the map. "She's almost made it to Pineville. That's all the way at the other end of the bay. Maybe she really is running away in a desperate ploy to keep the kittens."

We turned onto the main road and began the trek toward Pineville.

Charles took a pack of gum from the cupholder and offered me a piece before taking one for himself. "Why would she run away? I mean she has to know she'd eventually need to come back. Right?"

"To bribe me, maybe?" I sat back in my seat and watched the trees pass by my window.

My mean old boyfriend laughed at me. "Man, you're just letting everyone manipulate you today."

"Don't get used to it, and don't try anything," I warned in a growl.

He laughed again and turned on the car's radio. An upbeat pop song danced forth from the speakers, and we sang along in a horrible, no-talent duet. It gave us a nice break from all the kitten, cat, raccoon drama back home.

"Look!" I cried, just as we'd finished our third sing-along. "She's stopping!" I unclipped the phone and zoomed in on the map. "A Donut A Day?" I read the address label aloud. "Why would she drive so far just for some donuts?"

"Maybe A Donut A Day is to donuts as the Little Dog Diner is to lobster rolls. Worth the long drive."

My stomach growled at the thought of fresh cinnamon donuts straight from the oven. But no, this still didn't make sense even if it seemed delicious.

I returned the app to navigation mode and clipped it back into the holder. "She prefers to bake her own desserts, though, and she's never once mentioned this place to me."

"I'm sure it was just an oversight. Your nan always has a million things going on. It can be hard to keep track."

"Are you saying she told me and I forgot?" I grumped. "Oh, look! She's moving again!"

Nan's dot carried on for a few miles, then stopped again about five minutes later. I zoomed in but couldn't see any nearby businesses. It seemed Nan had chosen a residential area as her destination.

This time she stayed put until Charles and I were able to catch up.

Charles parked beside the curb behind Nan's gleaming red Audi. "I feel kind of out of place here," he mumbled as we both surveyed the neighborhood. Everything was well-kept but tiny—a far cry from my palatial manor home back in Glendale.

We emerged from his luxury sedan while a rusted-up beater rumbled down the road ahead of us.

"Who does Nan know here?" he asked as we watched the other car disappear around the block.

"I have no idea."

"Well, let's go find out."

We held hands as we walked up to the nearest house and pressed the doorbell. An exuberant cacophony of barks greeted us almost instantly—one clearly belonged to our Paisley, but the other was that of a much larger dog. Could this be the same Great Dane she'd bested in wrestling earlier that day?

It was Nan who opened the door. If she was surprised to see us there, she didn't show it.

"You might as well c'mon in," she said while a massive furry dog strained to push past her.

"Jasper, get back!" another voice called from inside the house, a much younger voice.

A woman about my age appeared and put the dog in a sit-stay. "Sorry," she said with an apologetic grin. "We're still working on Jasper's doorbell manners. Anyway... You must be Angie."

Who was this girl? And how did she know me?

"Mommy!" Paisley ran over the moment I stepped through the door and danced on her hindlegs. "Pick me up! Pick me up!"

I did as instructed, still confused out of my mind.

"Sorry. My name's Sunny. I should have started with that," the young woman said, letting go of her dog then wiping her hand off on her pantleg before offering it to me in greeting.

I let go of Charles's hand to accept it.

"Your grandma is friends with my neighbor who's kind of like a grandma to me and—"

"Just call me Nan, dear," Nan interjected while fussing with her hair in the hallway mirror. "Everyone else does."

"This is Charles," I said, reclaiming Charles's hand, so thankful we were in this together. "And you're right, I am Angie. Angie Russo. Um, are the kittens here by any chance?"

"Oh, yes! I was just picking out which one I wanted. It's so hard. They're all adorable!" she gushed.

I glanced toward Nan for an explanation.

She just shrugged. "I called my old friend Tilly to see if she knew anyone in need of a kitten, and she put me on to Sunny here."

As the girl nodded, a strand of dark hair shook loose from her messy braid. "Jasper needs a friend, but I'm afraid our place isn't quite big enough for a second dog."

"So you'd like to adopt a kitten?" I asked. How could such a tiny creature be a match for the massive, slobbery guy standing before me?

Sunny's bright blue eyes flashed with worry. "That's okay. Isn't it?"

"Of course, it's okay! I just wish Nan had told me before disappearing on us."

"Sorry about that. I was really excited, which is why she offered to come over straight away."

"I didn't even wait for Tilly," Nan supplied with a wink. "Although I'm still hoping she'll adopt one of our babies, too."

Sunny laughed. "I'll be sure to pass that on. Hey, now that you guys are here, could you help me decide on a kitten?"

"We'd be honored," Charles answered.

"Do I smell donuts?" I asked Nan before joining Charles, Sunny, and the kittens in the living room. My rumbling stomach was more than ready for a treat.

16

We spent the better part of the next hour at Sunny's. She ultimately chose the only gray kitten of the bunch and then immediately dubbed the little miss *Princess Muffin.*

While we were on the way out, Paisley confided in me, "I didn't want to say goodbye to any of my cat puppies."

I waited until Sunny had shut the door behind us to respond. "I know, sweetie. I am so sorry."

Much to my surprise, Paisley wagged her tail so hard her whole body shook. "That's okay, Mommy. I didn't want to say goodbye, but it made me feel good that Sunny and Jasper are so happy now. Do you think Princess Muffin will like living with them?"

I smiled and reached down to pat Paisley on the back. "I know she will."

"That's all any good Mommy can do. Prepare her cat puppies for the world and give them the best opportunities they can." The little dog's capacity to love never ceased to amaze me.

"You're a great mother, Paisley," I told her.

"You are, too, Mommy."

A wall of emotion crashed into me, and I couldn't help but tear up after receiving those tender words from Paisley. Luckily, I always kept a tissue stashed in my pocket during cold and flu season. I drew it out now and used it to wipe at my eyes.

"What's wrong?" Charles asked, concerned etched around the edges of his mouth.

"Nothing," I lied. How could I tell him that maybe I was readier for our future than I thought? Yes. Maybe I *could* be a wife and mother someday, because I already helped to raise one wonderful little doggie and one mostly okay cat.

"All right!" Nan waved to us from the driver's side of her little red sports coupe. "See you crazy kids back at home."

"Wait!" I trudged across the slushy road after my grandmother. "Why didn't you tell us where you were going before you left? And why didn't you answer your phone when we tried calling you?"

"Oh, sorry about that. I silenced it after the bootcamp instructor yelled at another gal for receiving a text alert. Seems I forgot to turn it back on after."

"But you called Sunny," I argued.

"No, I called *Tilly,* then she put me on to Sunny. And I used our landline, dear. Sometimes the simplest option is best." She rummaged around in her giant handbag until she found her phone and waved it in front me. "See. It's right here."

Unsurprisingly, her phone had accumulated so many unread notifications the list of them fell off the screen.

"Give me that." I grabbed the poor, neglected device from her hands and entered her highly secure passcode, *1-2-3-4.*

"It looks like you have several texts and missed calls from... um, *Diamond Guy?*" That was definitely a new one.

Nan blushed and took the phone back. "That's private."

"Who's Diamond Guy?" I teased, unable to suppress the giant smile that spread across my face.

She fluffed her hair, but it did little to distract from the deep blush that had taken over both cheeks. "It's just a new nickname we're trying out. After all, he does sell diamonds for a living."

"Oh my gosh. Is this how you and Mr. Gable flirt?" I broke apart laughing. Nan was usually so brazen with her friendships but acted completely different in her recent flirtations with the local jewelry shop owner.

"Hush up, you," she clucked. "You and Charles were no better in the start."

My smile had become stuck on my face. "Aren't you going to see what he wants?"

She jammed her phone back in her purse while shaking her head. "You know I'm a very private person."

I laughed right in her face. "Really? Since when?"

"Fine. I'll call him back now. Happy?" She grabbed her phone again and pressed the CALL button.

"Why not just check your messages?" I suggested as the line continued to ring.

"I don't have my voicemail set up. Don't need it, because I have an answering machine—"

"On the land line," I finished for her. "What about the texts?"

She ended the attempted call. Apparently Mr. Gable didn't have his voicemail set up, either. Old people are so funny sometimes.

Nan showed me her phone again. She did, indeed, have six new texts from Diamond Guy, but every single one said the same thing: *Hello, Dorothy. Please call me when you get the chance.*

Jeez. Diamond Guy needed some serious advice on flirting for the modern age. For starters, didn't he know that my grandmother preferred everyone call her Nan rather than her given name of Dorothy?

"There. That's done. Now can we please go home?" Nan turned her key over in the ignition to punctuate her request.

"I think Charles and I will just stop by Diamond Guy's on the way home." I snickered. "You're welcome to come with us."

"Goodbye, dear." Nan slammed the car door and sped off.

I returned to Charles with that same huge smile on my face.

"What's got you so smiley?" he asked, before giving me a quick peck on the cheek.

"Nan and her boyfriend. They're just so adorable."

"I didn't realize she was seeing anyone."

"She's not exactly, but remember all the flirting happening between her and Mr. Gable over New Year's Eve?"

He chuckled at the memory. "Do I ever."

"Good, because we need to stop by his store and see him, and I might need your help playing Cupid."

"Aren't we supposed to be focusing on the kittens today?"

I shrugged. "We've run out of clues as to where they and the blood came from, the vet declared them healthy, and both Nan and Paisley have agreed to find new homes for them. What more can we do at this point?"

He nodded. "But are you sure it's right to push them? Shouldn't we let those two get together in their own time?"

I scoffed at this. "Don't you remember how she was to me before we got together?"

"Oh, right." He winced, likely recalling how

Nan had forced an awkward confrontation between him and my other potential suitor.

"With that in mind, then yes. We should definitely meddle," he agreed. "Turnabout is fair play and all that. Um, could you give me the address to his shop? I've never headed that way from so far out and I'd hate to waste time taking the scenic route."

"It's downtown," I reminded him. I knew he was still relatively new to town, but surely he couldn't have forgotten that.

"I know, but the GPS likes it better when I give her an exact address."

I raised an eyebrow in question. *"Her?"*

"Yeah. Her name is Carla," he said as if naming his GPS was the most normal thing in the world.

"Hey, that's the same name as..." As my raccoon's Nerf gun. Awkward. "Never mind."

"What?"

"Seriously never mind. Anyway, I have the address for you. Are you ready?"

"Shoot."

"It's 1385 Third Street. Oh my gosh!" I shouted, practically dropping my phone in my lap from the shock.

Charles glanced about in panic. "What? What?"

"Look at this," I said thrusting my phone in his face. I'd pulled up the picture of the partially obscured address label and sure enough… we had a match.

Charles got it right away. "That looks an awful lot like the address you just gave me."

My smile was back and wider than ever. "It does. Doesn't it?"

"Let's go."

harles and I completed the drive to downtown Glendale in record time. Of course, neither of us had ever come this way from Pineville so it was easy for us to set a new record.

No sooner had we parked than Nan pulled her little red sports car into the space beside us.

"I hoped you were only kidding about interfering in my love life," she grumbled, getting out of her car and slamming the door behind her. "Luckily, I decided to come by just in case. You'll have to make whatever you plan on doing quick, because I'm not leaving those kittens for more than a few minutes."

I peered in the car window and saw the kittens

waiting in the carrier on the passenger side seat. Nan had even left the car running, presumably to keep the heat going for them.

"Let's go see what Diamond Guy is up to." Charles offered Nan his arm, but she refused to take it.

"You should have chosen the other guy," she mumbled in my direction as she stormed off across the parking lot.

Charles and I caught up with her in front of Mr. Gable's jewelry store, and the three of us entered together with Paisley following close at our heels.

"Hello, Dorothy!" Mr. Gable waved from behind the counter. "Hi, Angie. Charles."

We all said our hellos, and then the shopkeeper returned to his customers.

A mother-son pair stood before him examining engagement rings and occasionally asking to see one closer up.

"Congrats," Charles told the son who had rusty red hair and appeared to be somewhere in his mid-thirties.

The other man's skin turned a ruddy shade of red. "Not me." He jammed a finger his mother's direction. "Her."

His mother beamed at me and Charles. "Isn't it so great to finally find the one?" she asked us.

Charles pulled me to his side and gave me a kiss on the cheek, which made the newly engaged woman swoon with delight.

"We're just finishing up here, if you could give me a few more minutes," Mr. Gable said, his eyes focused only on Nan as they blinked an apology.

"I like it here," Paisley barked, drawing the engaged woman's attention.

"Oh my goodness. What an angel!" She dropped to her haunches and accepted excited kisses from the hyper Chihuahua.

"Mom," the woman's son nudged her impatiently. "That's not what we're here for."

"Oh, stop. The ring will wait. Give me a minute to say hello."

He sighed, but his mother didn't seem too bothered by it.

Mr. Gable used this opportunity to extricate himself from behind the counter. "Hello," he said to both me and Charles before saddling Nan with a giant hug. "What brings all three of you in? Is this about the kittens I left on your porch this morning?"

Ah-ha! I knew it!

Nan blinked in confusion. We hadn't yet gotten the chance to catch her up on the address label match-up. "*You* left them?"

"Of course. I'm sorry I didn't have the chance to clean them up. When I called, you didn't answer. I was in a hurry to get back for a customer appointment. I figured if anyone would know what to do with them, it would be you two."

"Wait." The female customer stopped petting Paisley and rose back to a standing position. "There are kittens?" she whispered reverently.

"Mom, we need to focus on—"

"Oh, shush. You're not the one who gets to make the rules." She waved him off, then approached us with wide, shining eyes. "So about those kittens?"

"Would you like to meet them?" Nan asked with a chuckle. "I left them in the car for a minute. Didn't expect to be here long."

"It sounds like the perfect wedding gift. My fiancé John is quite the animal lover but hasn't been able to keep any pets in his apartment."

Her son tugged at her sleeve in a gesture reminiscent of a much younger child. "But, Mom, I'm allergic to cats."

"Then I guess it's finally time for you to move

out and establish your own home," she told him with a pointed glare.

"I'll just go get them," Nan said before sweeping back into the cold outside.

The woman followed after Nan and her son followed after her.

"Where did the kittens come from?" I asked Mr. Gable, eager to finally get the answers I'd craved all day. "And why were they covered in blood?

"A frightening sight. Wasn't it?" He shook his head and spoke in the direction of his feet. "I found them in the alley when I was walking in to work."

"The one just outside?" Charles asked, picking up Paisley and allowing her to lick his face.

"Not this one, no. I like to park in the far lot to get a bit of exercise. Plus the fresh air helps wake me up in the mornings. When I spotted the kittens, I picked up the pace, grabbed a box and left a note on the door to let my customers know I'd be a few minutes late opening today, then I went back to get the kittens and drove them straight over to your place. I tried calling Dorothy, but..." He shrugged again.

"I know. She's had her phone off all day."

"Speaking of Nan," Charles edged in. "I've

heard she's looking for a plus-one on Valentine's Day."

The old jeweler's breathing suddenly became labored. I half-expected him to a pull an inhaler from his pocket and take a hit. "Is that so? A plus-one for what?"

"Well, actually she doesn't," I began to explain.

Charles squeezed my hand to get me to stop.

He cleared his throat. "It's a beautiful evening she has planned. It starts with an intimate hike along the coastline. After about half an hour, you'll find yourselves at a secluded ice castle built especially just for the two of you. You'll have just enough time for a quick snowball fight before a private chef will treat you to a freshly prepared meal suited perfectly to your individual tastes. Finally, the night will end with dancing under the stars to a string quartet playing only the greatest '80s hits."

Mr. Gable looked like he might be moved to cry. "That sounds wonderful. She did all that for me?"

Charles squeezed my hand again. "She did, but I think she's nervous to make things official by asking you to accompany her. You should do the honors."

I gave an encouraging nod. "Yeah, I bet she'd say yes."

"Okay, I'll do that," Mr. Gable promised.

We made small talk with Mr. Gable as we waited for Nan, Paisley, and the customers to return. I knew Charles had planned that date for me, and as amazing as that special evening sounded, it meant even more to me that he'd given it all up to help two elderly people start their own love story.

Boy, did I have a keeper or what?

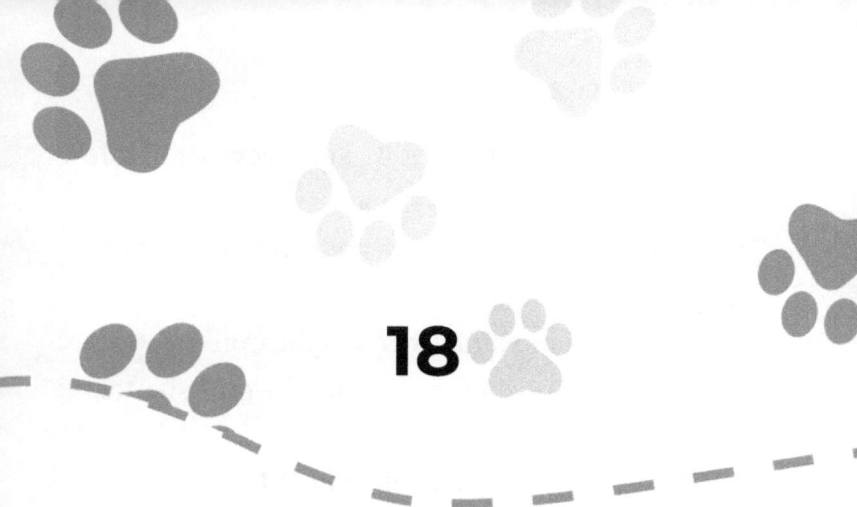

18

The woman in the jewelry store ended up adopting two of the kittens, a boy and a girl. She and Nan exchanged phone numbers, and she also promised to text updates and pictures every single day.

That meant we only had two of the original five kittens left with us now, one boy and one girl. At the rate things were going, we'd probably have homes for them by nightfall.

"You wouldn't happen to know anyone in need of their own personal feline overlord. Would you?" I asked Mr. Gable once mother, son, and kittens had departed.

He sighed. "I wish I could take them off your hands, but I fear E.B. would never forgive me."

I'd met his pet rabbit, E.B., and knew Mr. Gable was definitely correct in his assessment. The poor little mite was afraid of any and everything, especially predators like cats.

"Well..." Nan shifted her weight from one foot to the other. "We should probably be off," she told the ground.

Charles exchanged a meaningful glance with Mr. Gable, while I clasped my hands and waited for the magic to happen.

"Dorothy?" Mr. Gable said, causing her to look up.

She lifted Paisley from the floor and nuzzled the little dog to her chest, using Paisley as her own personal security blanket. All this shyness was so unlike my grandmother!

"Yes, Grant?" she mumbled into Paisley's fur after taking one slow, steady breath.

His voice quavered as he asked, "Would you like to spend Valentine's Day together?"

Nan jerked her head a little. "Sure. You mean, as friends?"

No, Nan! No! I wanted to shout but didn't.

Mr. Gable shot an anxious glance Charles's way, who nodded his encouragement.

"No," the nervous shopkeeper said at last. "I

meant as in a date. Our first date."

Nan blushed as she continued to stroke Paisley for a couple silent moments. At last, a smile blossomed on her face. "I'd like that," she declared just like the heroine always did in old-timey movies.

"Me, too," Mr. Gable said. He looked as if he'd just won first prize in life. In a way, he had. As trying as my nan could sometimes be, she was still my very favorite person in the entire world. I couldn't blame the besotted jeweler for feeling the same way.

"I should be going now, though." Nan backed away, accidentally bumping into one of the jewelry counters in the process.

"See you soon, Mr. Gable!" I called while pushing my clumsy nan toward the exit. "Bye!"

Once outside, Nan straightened her back and ran her fingers through her hair. "Well, that was rather unexpected."

"Was it, though?" I teased, making my voice high and sarcastic. "You were just telling me this morning that you enrolled in booty boot camp precisely because Mr. Gable—"

"Angie!" Nan shouted and gave me a light slap on the arm. "That's private! Besides I don't want Grant to overhear that."

"What does booty boot camp have to do with Mr. Gable?" Paisley asked, tilting her head to the side.

"I'll tell you when you're older," I whispered while scratching her head.

"Are we going home now?" the Chihuahua asked as we all moved toward the parking lot.

"You, Nan, and the kittens are," I answered. "Charles and I still have a bit of work left to do here."

"Okay, byeeeee!" she sang as Nan practically floated away.

Charles turned to me once we'd seen Nan and the animals off and asked, "The blood?"

I nodded. "Mr. Gable told us where he found it and the kittens. Now all we have to do is go take a look for ourselves."

He motioned for me to go ahead. "Lead the way," he said, placing his hand at the small of my back.

Downtown Glendale wasn't very large, which meant it took us less than ten minutes to reach the other end. From the far parking lot, we headed toward the nearest alley.

"We probably should have kept Paisley with us," I admitted, kicking myself for not realizing that earlier. "She'd have been able to sniff this out for us in a heartbeat."

Charles paused midstep. "Should we go get her?"

"*Nah.* We just have to trace and retrace our steps until something turns up."

"What are we looking for exactly? Bloody pawprints?"

I kept my eyes on the ground before me, studying it closely so I wouldn't miss anything. "Yeah, that's probably our best bet."

"Look there." He pointed toward a big green dumpster that hadn't been properly sealed to keep animals out. Not only were there little red pawprints at the base, but something inside created an ominous rustling sound as soon as I locked eyes on the dumpster.

"Stay back," Charles warned me, putting his arm out to stop me before continuing forward. It was nice he wanted to protect me, but Charles was forgetting one very important piece of information here—*I* was the one who could talk to animals.

"Who's in there?" I called. It had already been a very long winter, and the local wildlife often got desperate as the cold months continued to bear down on the region.

For all I knew, there could be a fox, coyote, lynx, or some other kind of potentially dangerous predator in there. I'd never spoken to any members of those species, so didn't know how easy—*or how difficult*—they might be to negotiate with. And that worried me.

"Hellooooo!" I called again. "You in the dumpster. Come out and nobody gets hurt."

Of course, I would never hurt an animal, but I needed some kind of leverage if I were to protect Charles.

A large raggedy looking dog popped his head out of the dumpster. His wiry coat was also matted with blood around the muzzle. "Don't hurt me," he whined. "I was only trying to grab a quick bite."

Relieved, I closed the distance between myself and the dumpster. "My name's Angie. What's yours?"

When the dog whimpered, his half-cocked ears went back against his head. "I don't have a name. You need a home to have a name, and I've never had one of those."

"I could give you one if you'd like," I offered with a gentle voice. The poor thing.

"A home?" he squeaked in surprise. "I would love nothing more."

"I meant a name, but I suppose I can find you a home, too. First can you help me with something?"

"Anything," he barked excitedly, his tongue now lolling from the side of his mouth.

"What are you eating in there?" I asked, craning my neck but failing to see into the dumpster.

"I'll show you!" he shouted, then dived back into the dumpster and tossed a bloody carcass in my direction. Luckily, it missed hitting me.

"Ewww. What is that?"

"Not ewww. *Yum.*" The stray dog licked his chops. "I hardly ever find something this good to eat."

"What is it?" I asked in disgust. As much as I liked to be polite, it was hard to ignore the churning in my stomach at the smell and sight of his half-eaten meal.

"Looks like some kind of roadkill," Charles said.

"Why is it in the dumpster?"

"Good question. Do you think this is what the kittens got into before Mr. Gable found them?"

"Kittens? You mean cat puppies?" the dog asked, tilting his head to one side and studying us with teary, dark brown eyes.

"Yes, cat puppies," I confirmed with a smile.

"They were the ones who first found this delicious feast, but then some man took them away before they could finish, and I took over."

There.

That was the last piece we'd needed to piece together the entire story of the mysterious doorstep kittens. No wonder they had been so hungry. Their first meal in who-knows-how-long had been interrupted.

"Thanks for your help," I told the dog and then added, "By the way, how do you like the name Digger? You know, because when I first met you, you were digging in the trash?"

"It's perfect!" he barked enthusiastically. "I'm part Airedale terrier on my mother's side, and—boy —do our kind love to dig."

A nameless stray no more, he jumped out of the dumpster and trotted to my side, his tail wagging mightily with each step.

"Then it's definitely perfect." I patted him between the ears as they appeared to be the cleanest part of him. "Hi, Digger. It's nice to meet you. Now come with us, and we'll see what we can do about finding you a home."

19

Luckily, Mr. Gable had a tarp leftover from when he'd painted his shop that summer. He was also more than happy to lend it to us so that we could take Digger back to my house while avoiding the spread of blood, dirt, and trash all over the back seat of my car.

Paisley immediately took the new, much larger dog under her wing. She came running straight up to him and stood on her hindlegs to complete the requisite butt sniff.

"Hi. My name's Paisley!" she shouted while allowing him to bend down and sniff hers.

"My name's Digger," the other dog answered proudly, finally having a name to share.

"I will teach you everything about being a

pet!" Paisley promised, then she and Digger disappeared outside. Digger didn't fit through our pet door, so I had to open the human door to let him out.

"Where are the kittens?" I asked Nan, surprised they weren't in the living room with her.

"Upstairs with Octavius in the fish room," she answered casually between sips of tea.

"Don't let him hear you call it that," I warned with a quick eyeroll. "Have you found any of the other kittens homes yet?"

"Not yet, but I may have a couple leads." She smiled over the rim of her teacup before taking another slow sip.

"Think you could find one for Digger, too?"

"I'll see what I can do," she promised, setting her cup back on the table. "Would you like some tea, too, dear?"

I shook my head. "No, thanks."

"Not you." She turned to my boyfriend. "You. How about it?"

"I'm not really—"

"Oh, come now. You and I need to have a little chat," she pressed, already up and heading toward the kitchen.

Understanding that I'd been dismissed, I headed

up the stairs and let myself into Octo-Cat's room. I needed to check on the kittens, anyway.

The vision that greeted me practically took my breath away. Our two remaining kittens lay snuggled up against Octo-Cat as all three cats napped.

I was just about to turn around and head out, when Octo-Cat's wide amber eyes blinked open and he whispered, "Wait."

He carefully extricated himself from his slumber companions without waking either. "I wanted to talk to you about something," he told me once he'd successfully come to stand by my side. "Let's go out into the hall."

"What's up?" I asked curiously

"Those little guys aren't so bad, you know. It was hard when they first got here and were pouncing everywhere, but truth be told I've liked having them around," he revealed with a wistful sigh.

"Are you saying you want to keep them?"

He hissed at this. "Eeeesh, no! Nothing so extreme. But having them here reminded me of my own kittenhood. Have I told you that I was one of seven?"

"You may have mentioned it a time or two." *Or twenty.*

"Today has got me thinking about my own brothers and sisters. I haven't seen them since Ethel adopted me all those years ago."

"You must miss them." I ran my hand along his back, hoping he'd appreciate the comfort of the gesture rather than attacking me for it.

He leaned into my hand and purred. "Yes and no. I'm definitely happier being an only cat, but I do wonder if they turned out as awesome as I have."

"So you want to track them down?"

My cat nodded. "I think I do."

"I guess it makes sense to use our P.I. skills to help ourselves every once in a while."

He smiled and gave me a paws up. "Exactly."

"Are you sure you don't want to keep one of the kittens?" I tried again. I liked seeing this softer side of him. Maybe having a long-term kitty companion would help him mellow out.

He shuddered and turned his backside to me. "Completely."

"Okay. Well, I'll let you get back to your cat nap, then."

"Thank you, Angela," he said before running back through the door I'd just opened. I couldn't blame him for wanting to find his long-lost family. After all, I was still trying to do the same thing for myself—and finally meeting my cousin Mags had definitely changed my life for the better.

Knowing now that the kittens were in good paws with Octo-Cat, I headed back downstairs to ask Charles for a quick favor.

"Would you mind heading to the store for me? I need large dog breed food and some steak."

He took one last slurp from his tea, then asked, "How much steak?"

I made a tally in my head. "Um, twenty-two should do it."

Charles laughed. "Time to pay your debts, I see."

"Yes, and if you happen to find a TV, Nerf gun, or nunchucks while you're there, you know what to do."

"What about the lobster rolls?" he asked with one eyebrow raised.

"Those can wait for a few days. We're having steak for dinner tonight."

While Charles was at the store, I planned to give Digger a bath, but first I needed a short break so that I could catch my breath. I took a seat by Nan, who was busy typing into her phone and smiling like a fool in love.

"Let me guess. *Diamond Guy?*" I teased.

Nan clucked her tongue. "I have much more going on in my life than that," she chided.

"Still it must be pretty exciting to have your first date on the calendar at last?"

Nan frowned for a few seconds before transitioning back into a smile. "I only wish I would have had a few more sessions of booty boot camp first, but—yes—I am very excited."

"If you're not talking to Mr. Gable, then who are you texting?" I said, trying to catch a glimpse of her screen. "You're not cheating on him already?"

She looked sad rather than angry. "Oh, dear. I am many things, but a cheater, I am not. You should know me better than that."

"Well?" I prompted when she still hadn't answered my first question. "Who are you chatting with, then?"

She rolled her eyes. "You're so nosey sometimes. You know that?"

"I learned it from the best." I winked, and she winked back.

"That was my good friend, Gertie."

Ahh, Gertie. I'd never actually met her, but I'd taken several jogs with her muttsky Cujo. Cujo had also helped to save my life last month, so he rated very high in my books and so did his owner, Gertie.

Nan continued along. "Remember how she was having trouble exercising Cujo since her grandkids went off to college?"

I nodded.

"I've just suggested she adopt a playmate for him. You and I will keep exercising Cujo as we do, but a second dog could give him some nice company during the day. Wouldn't you say?"

I gasped with excitement. "Digger?"

"Digger," she confirmed.

"That's great," I cried and gave her a tight hug.

"I also have a lead on a home for the last two kittens," Nan revealed. Man, she was good at this. Perhaps she should volunteer at the local animal shelter for more than just fundraising events.

"Really? Who?" I asked, so happy for all the animals who'd found new homes that day.

She shook her head and wagged a finger at me. "I don't want to say until it's a sure thing, but I promise to tell you as soon as I can."

I stretched my arms overhead, then forced myself to my feet. "I better get Digger in the bath."

"Before you go, I take back what I said."

I stared at her blankly. "Take back what?"

"I'm really glad you chose Charles. He's a good man."

"You know," I stated, referring to the fact that Charles had so willingly given up his special Valentine's surprise in order to offer it to Nan and Mr. Gable.

She nodded. "Thank you both for that. Although if it's not too late, I might ask the string quartet to play something other than '80s covers."

20

After our twenty-two-steak dinner, Charles said goodbye and headed back to his house. I felt bad that our "relaxing" day together had become so hectic and that he'd also sacrificed his big Valentine's surprise, but I vowed to make up for it by planning a few special surprises of my own.

By the time Friday rolled around, I had my work cut out for me.

I started with a quick good morning call to Charles, who would be working until early evening. I spent the morning with Nan and Paisley until they departed for one of her community art classes.

The last two kittens had gone to their new

homes the night before, which meant Octo-Cat and I had the house to ourselves for the next few hours.

"Happy Valentine's Day," I crooned as I placed a giant box onto the floor in front of him.

His eyes lit up as he beheld the cardboard behemoth. "For me?" he gasped with obvious delight.

"Yup. And there's even a surprise *inside* the box."

He raised a paw to his chest. "Double presents? I'm touched."

It had been so hard to keep this surprise from him for the last few days, and I couldn't wait another minute for the big reveal. "Well, go on and open it up," I urged.

Octo-Cat jumped into the box, then popped his head back out with a satin blue swatch of fabric clenched between his jaws. "What is it?" he mumbled, unsure.

"It's a bowtie," I explained. "I figured you could wear it on your video date with Grizabella this afternoon."

"It matches her beautiful sapphire eyes," he said after setting it carefully on the floor.

"Yes, it does. And if you take another look inside, you'll find a green bowtie as well."

He narrowed his eyes at me, then cocked his

head slightly to the side—a sure sign that Paisley was beginning to rub off on him just a little bit.

"Why green?" he asked.

I put a hand over my smiling mouth and waited for it to sink in.

Octo-Cat swooned with delight less than a minute later. "Green. Glorious green! Does this mean...?"

I picked up where he left off. "Yes, I'm taking you to visit Grizabella for St. Patrick's Day. That is, if you still want to go."

He zipped up and down the stairs in a rare show of kitty zoomies, then came back to rest at my feet. I reached out to pet him, but before I could, he licked my fingertips. "You are a very good human, and I love you, Angela."

I stroked his soft back. "Awww, I love you, too. Now are you ready to FaceTime with Grizabella?"

"Yes! Yes! Yes!"

I fastened the blue bowtie to his collar and showed him what he looked like in the selfie mode of my phone. "I am a very handsome cat. Aren't I?"

I nodded my endorsement. "Grizabella is very lucky to have you."

"And I'm lucky to have you," he said sweetly before zooming away to call his girlfriend.

My heart melted a little at that. Getting love from any cat—but especially Octo-Cat—was a rare treat, and I planned to savor every single second.

* * *

At five o'clock on the dot, I pulled into the parking lot outside Charles's law firm. He wasn't expecting me, but that was part of the surprise.

It felt strange being back in the location where our love story had first begun—and also where I'd almost died and then woke up with the strange ability to talk to Octo-Cat. Yes, Longfellow & Associates had given me so much during my brief tenure there—love, friendship, a cat, a home, and access to an impressive trust fund—and for all of it, I would forever be grateful.

But today wasn't about the associates, it was about Charles Longfellow, III, and me.

When he saw me enter the office, he jumped up from his desk and wrapped me in his arms. "What are you doing here? I was just about to sign off for the day and come to see you."

"Kidnapping you. Now let's go."

"Sure. Just let me turn off—"

"Nope. Just lock the door and come with me.

There's no time to waste." I grabbed his hand and pulled him along.

We settled into my car, and I began the drive.

"Where are we going?" he asked me with an enormous grin.

I shrugged, keeping my eyes straight ahead. "It's not as fancy as what you had planned, but it's very us."

"Tell me. Tell me!" he whined playfully.

I took a deep breath and shook my head. "I won't tell you what we're doing, but I'll explain why."

"Okay, hit me."

I licked my lips before continuing. I'd practiced this a couple times but still worried it would come out wrong.

"Well, we first met at the law firm, which is why we started there today. A lot of people meet at work, but our relationship has always been a bit different as you so rightly pointed out last weekend. And even though you'd wanted to spend a relaxing, romantic day together, we ended up spending that day in a very *us* way—by throwing all our plans out the window and then helping those who needed it most. Think about it. When we first became friends, we got Brock Calhoun acquitted for murder and reunited a lost, little dog with his human. When we first became more, we saved Octo-Cat from a kidnapper and protected his trust fund from angry relatives. Last weekend, we ended up finding five abandoned kittens and one stray dog their forever homes."

Charles nodded along, then frowned. "Yes. I guess you're right about that. Do you ever wish we spent more time doing normal boyfriend-girlfriend stuff?"

"No way!" I protested. "I love you, and I love us. Exactly as we are."

"I love you, too." He squeezed my shoulder and leaned in to plant a kiss on my cheek, then asked, "So what are we doing for Valentine's Day?"

"Haha, nice try," I teased. "Don't worry, though. We're almost there."

Ten minutes later, we arrived at our very favorite restaurant, the Little Dog Diner all the way over in Misty Harbor.

"This restaurant has always been special to us, too," Charles observed as we approached the entrance hand in hand. "Remember when we came here after catching the real Hayes murderer?"

"I do. And do you remember who came with us?"

Just then we caught sight of Nan, Mr. Gable, and my parents as they waved from a big booth by the window.

Charles turned to me with a curious look. "I thought Nan and Grant were going on the date I'd originally planned for us."

I squeezed his hand and rested my head on his shoulder for a moment. "Remember about helping people in need? Those two are still too nervous to be alone together, so we're going to help break the ice. And you know another thing about us? We love to be with the people we love, so why not be with them on Valentine's Day? Well, for a little while, at least."

"We're just staying for a quick drink." My mom looked ravishing in a pink cable-knit sweater. I swear, only she could look glamorous in such simple winter attire. She gave me a tight hug and then kissed me on either cheek.

"Thank you again for setting up the ice castle dinner for us," my father said, giving my boyfriend a manly hug and several fast pats on the back.

"We're sharing," I revealed the favorite part of my plan with a smile. "My parents are doing the dinner, and you and I get the string quartet."

Charles laughed, and I jabbed him in the ribs.

"What? You think I'm going to pass-up a romantic starlight dance to all my favorite '80s classics?"

"No, I know you better than that." After a moment, he asked, "You said that we were sharing the date I'd planned. What part do Nan and Grant get?"

"They're going to have the snowball fight, of course. They need something more light-hearted to help them get comfortable dating again. It's been a long time for both of them." I eyed the new couple, glad to see they were holding hands across the booth. Maybe they didn't need quite as much help as I'd expected.

"Take a seat, you two," Nan urged, motioning for Charles and me to slide into the large booth with one hand while still hanging tight to Mr. Gable's hand with the other.

The waitress came over and handed out waters all around. "I see the rest of your party has arrived. Are you ready to order?"

"Four lobster rolls for here and two to go," I said as my mouth began to water in anticipation.

"Oh, that's nice, sweetie," Mom said, "But your dad and I don't need anything to take home."

"So just four for here?" the waitress asked, her pen raised over the little Steno pad in her grip.

"And two to go," I confirmed with a sharp nod.

After she'd left, I whispered to Mom, "They're not for you. They're for paying the rest of my debts to a certain cat and his raccoon friend."

It's time for a big road trip with Angie, Octo-Cat and the gang... and for their whackiest adventure yet!

Get your copy of *Legal Seagull* so that you can keep reading this series today!

Pssst... If you absolutely loved this book and want even more, make sure you **sign up for Molly's newsletter**. When you do, you'll receive an exclusive digital prize pack, including a free book!

WHAT'S NEXT?

Just as I was beginning to think we'd never find the last missing member of our long-lost family, a seagull named Bravo shows up with both a promise and a threat.

He claims he's been watching me for a long time—even before I gained my strange ability to talk to animals. He also says that if I help settle a dispute between warring flocks, then he'll personally take me to see the one person I've been all but dying to meet. If I refuse to help, however, he'll send an army of mercenary woodpeckers to destroy my house. Yikes!

Unfortunately, I've already promised Octo-Cat that I'll take him on a cross-country trip to visit his girl-friend out in Colorado. With Nan and I on the road, it falls to Charles and Pringle to investigate in our absence.

Will they be able to solve the case according to the flock's satisfaction? What shocking secrets has Nan been keeping from me now? And will I be able to survive more than 70 hours in the car with my complaining kitty?

The mysteries abound in our most unusual adventure yet.

LEGAL SEAGULL is now available.

Get your copy so that you can keep reading this series today!

SNEAK PEEK
LEGAL SEAGULL

t all started with a coffee maker that should have been tossed into the dumpster years ago. One fated zap from that thing, and I reawakened with the strange ability to speak with animals.

Ever since then, my life has been full of four-legged chatter. You'd think being able to understand animals would mean that I'd know more about the world around me, but instead I find myself knowing less and less as I'm tossed into one mystery after the other.

I guess that's why I set up shop as a private investigator...

Oh, hi. My name's Angie Russo, and I'd be remiss not to mention that my partner in solving crime is none other than my tabby cat, Octavius Maxwell Ricardo Edmund Frederick Fulton Russo, Esq, P.I. And much to his chagrin, I've taken to calling him Octo-Cat for short.

When Octo-Cat entered my life, he brought the first of many mysteries and a giant trust fund from his previous owner, for which I am now the guarantor. It pays our monthly bills and then some—including the giant Blueberry Bay manor house that he tricked me into buying. It's a good thing his previous owner hooked us up because we've earned exactly zero dollars for our investigative efforts to date.

My grandmother, Nan, lives with us and uses her retirement funds to pitch in, even though I tell her not to. She keeps our kitchen stocked with fresh baked goods and our walls decorated with all kinds of quirky homemade art projects—yeah, she's worked in everything from metal to hand-spun silk. She's a bit of a character, but we can always count on Nan to keep things interesting for us all.

Another roommate of ours is Paisley, the mostly black tri-color Chihuahua Nan rescued from the shelter last year. Paisley is an unfailing optimist and eternal source of joy. She makes a strong contrast to our backyard neighbor, Pringle the unrelentingly irritating and frequently villainous raccoon.

You probably won't believe me, but everything I'm about to tell you is true about Pringle. He has two treehouses with two big-screen TVs. He also has zero regard for anyone's privacy, especially mine. I've recently caught him snooping on my phone and even recording a video of me for submission to his favorite reality show. Ugh, I know. Here's hoping I don't get selected for that particular unwanted privilege.

My parents work in news, and my boyfriend Charles is the senior partner at the law firm where I used to work before giving up the glamorous paralegal life to become a full-time P.I... Or if you were to ask Pringle, "full-time unemployed."

I realize the raccoon must seem like an all-around horrible neighbor based on my descriptions so far, but in truth, I just think he's cranky. After all, he's the only one around here who hasn't found love.

That's right.

Nan is now seeing the local jeweler, Grant Gable, and they are just adorable together. Meanwhile I've got Charles, and my parents have each other. Even Octo-Cat maintains a very serious long-distance relationship with minor Instagram influencer and former show cat Grizabella the gorgeous Himalayan.

True, Paisley is without any romantic attachment, but that doesn't bother the spritely pup one bit. Mostly because things rarely ever do.

Even though Pringle won't admit to being lovelorn, he has taken to calling his Nerf gun "Carla" and stroking it lovingly whenever he thinks no one is looking.

Things have gotten so out of hand with that Nerf gun of his that I've now inadvertently agreed to let my cat wield nunchucks to protect himself—and, in theory, *me*. This has only led to more slapstick violence and a fair number of bruised shins on my part.

He's really not good with them.

Probably because he has to keep one part in his mouth while swinging the other as he stands on his hind legs and awkwardly twists his neck to the side. I think he's actually hurt himself more than he's managed to get me and Pringle.

I also don't think either of them needs a weapon to navigate our daily suburban life, but maybe that's just me.

Thankfully, I'll be getting a break from trigger-happy Pringle this week as I take Octo-Cat on a cross-country road trip to visit his beloved Grizabella in Colorado. Yes, it's a long drive from Maine, but Nan is coming along to share it with me, seeing as Octo-Cat still refuses to get on a plane.

Also, the last time we took a train, we wound up with a murder on our hands, so driving just felt like a better way to go this time around.

We're leaving bright and early the day after tomorrow, and as much as I initially didn't want to take this trip, I'm looking forward to the reprieve from everyday life.

Let's just hope nothing too crazy happens before then...

Famous last words. Am I right?

I'd just settled into my favorite window seat with a steaming mug of coffee in one hand and my eReader in the other when Octo-Cat came sauntering into the room, a single sheet of lined paper hanging from his mouth.

"Eeeh muh et," he mumbled in my direction, his tail already flicking wildly even though I'd not yet done anything to disappoint him.

"Whatever it is, can it wait until later?" I asked. Unfortunately, I already knew what his answer would be.

He spat the paper onto the floor and glared at me with those unsettling amber eyes of his. "No. It can't wait. We're almost out of time as it is. Pick that up," he commanded with a sneer.

I set my eReader down on the bench seat and walked my coffee over to my desk, then returned to grab the paper my cat had presented to me so unceremoniously.

Octo-Cat plopped onto his butt and watched with obvious disdain, but that was life with a cat for you. "That's my list of necessities."

I turned the paper over in my hands, then shook my head. "But it's blank."

"You better get writing then," Octo-Cat said with a triple flick of his tail before launching into his long-winded soliloquy. "First I'll need my bowties, both green and blue. I also need a new one that's gold to match my eyes."

"But your eyes aren't—"

"Are you writing this down?" he snapped with a scowl that brooked no further argument.

Right.

I raced to my desk as he continued to rattle off

his demands. With a red ink pen now in hand, I scrawled furiously but just couldn't keep up. "A copy of Dr. Roman's Guide to... um... Could you repeat that, please?"

My cat groaned, proving I'd disappointed him yet again. "Dr. Roman's Guide to Romance. In audio. Pay attention."

Ten minutes later, Octo-Cat had finally finished dictating his list. It filled both sides of the paper he'd brought me, and I'd even had to resort to scribbling the last few items on the back of my hand.

Well, it looked like I had my work cut out for me—and my day stolen from me.

"Are you sure you need all of this for our trip?" I asked in disbelief. "Some of this isn't exactly easy to find."

Octo-Cat nodded pertly. "I'm sure."

"But—"

"I'll be in my room if you need me." He turned tail and sauntered away.

Remind me again why I was doing this huge nice thing for him when he couldn't even bother to be the tiniest bit grateful?

It was like the more time I spent with my cat, the less I actually understood him. Maybe this road trip wouldn't be so relaxing, after all.

. . .

LEGAL SEAGULL is now available.

Get your copy so that you can keep reading this series today!

THE LITTLE DOG DINER

Curious about those lobster rolls Angie, Charles, Nan, and Octo-Cat love so much? They're from the Little Dog Diner, of course!

The Little Dog Diner is actually a sister series to Pet Whisperer P.I., and it's written by my very good friend Emmie Lyn. Sometimes places and characters cross over, but each series can be read totally on its own. They're way more fun together, though!

Now's a great time to catch up with LDD, because Emmie Lyn's new series, the Mint Chocolate Chip Mysteries, will be coming this spring—and it includes cross-over characters and places from both series.

You've already met its stars, too. Sunny,

Jasper, and Princess Muffin from *Lawless Litter* will be coming back for much more!

So catch up with them this Spring and dig into Little Dog Diner right now. Here's the first chapter of *Mixing Up Murder* to get you started... Enjoy!

* * *

"Why did I ever let you talk me into going to Ray's funeral?"

I didn't really expect my best friend, Lily, to answer me. She just gave me one of her looks. The one that talked me into spending a beautiful Monday morning attending a service at Two Wilde Funeral Home for someone I never even liked.

As though I had nothing better to do.

But... what do you do when your best friend needs you at an unpleasant affair? You put on your best little black dress, hold her hand and your nose, and hope for the best.

"Dani," Lily said, tenderly tucking one of my wayward curls behind my ear. My attempt to control my mass of auburn hair with a tiny silver hair clip failed miserably. Several curlicues always refused to cooperate. "Thanks for coming with me," she said in her musical voice. She completely ignored my discomfort and slipped her arm in mine. "I can't believe Ray died before the divorce became final." Then she maneuvered me toward the funeral home.

We took the steps up to the columned entrance of Two Wilde two at a time, late as usual because Lily got hung up worrying how she looked. She thought black made her long, blonde hair fade to a washed-out cream. I had to talk her out of an electric blue, figure-hugging sheath. "Sure, it makes your hair look like a crown of spun gold," I told her. "But you'll never live down the snide *merry widow* jokes in this town.

As far as her comment about her husband's death was concerned, I should say I was shocked, but I couldn't, because I wasn't.

Lily's soon to be ex-husband had been a worthless piece of scum as a husband, but on paper, he owned a lot of real estate in Misty Harbor, Maine, the picturesque town where we lived. Now everything would go to Lily. I couldn't be happier for her. And, I admit, I was a teensy bit jealous. She was set for life. And me? I'd be working my fingers off feeding the locals at the Little Dog Diner for, well, forever.

Don't get me wrong. I loved our diner. Yes, our — my grandma, Rose Mackenzie who owned the building and took care of the books, and Lily and I who did the day to day cooking and serving— had our own business, the Little Dog Diner. So, Lily wasn't just my best friend, but my business partner as well. I had an interest in her future, but who could blame her for choosing financial freedom over working? Um, no one.

I pulled the heavy wood door of Two Wilde Funeral Home open, pasted an appropriately somber expression on my face, smoothed any wrinkles out of my black dress, and followed my friend inside.

The door clicked shut behind us and all heads turned in our direction. A few gasps and whispers by Ray's family along the lines of, "I can't believe Lily brought Danielle Mackenzie," followed those head turns, but we stared straight ahead, locked our arms, and made our way to the casket.

An open casket.

Surrounded by white lilies.

"You didn't warn me about that," I hissed in Lily's ear as I jabbed her in the side, harder than I intended.

She winced. "Would you have come?" she whispered back.

"Of course not." We were three steps away from looking at the dead face of Raymond Lemay, and I didn't know if I'd make it without losing my blueberry muffin. Lily dragged me by the arm, reluctant as I was, up the aisle to the casket. I closed my eyes and let her blindly pull me to the spot I didn't want to be near under any circumstance. The sweet scent from the lilies around the casket was so strong I wanted to fan my hand in front of my face or rush outside to suck in fresh air. I didn't do either.

"This is the best he's ever looked," Lily whispered. "You won't believe it, Dani. His face is actually handsome now that he's relaxed. Open your eyes."

Against my better judgment, I cracked open one eye maybe an eighth of an inch. Then I closed it quickly, took a breath and opened it a sliver again. And held it open. "Okay, not as gruesome as I expected," I admitted.

I opened both eyes and blinked. "Who knew a dead guy could look this good," I said when I was sure my breakfast would stay put. "He looks like he's sleeping peacefully." Then something caught my eye.

Like almost blinding me. "What's that sparkling on his chest?" I whispered to Lily, after checking to be sure no one was watching, I reached in and snatched the item off Ray's shirt. I caught a quick look at what I held in my hand, and saw it was just an earring probably from some weepy relative leaning too far over the body. I tucked it in my pocket to deal with later.

Together, we stared at the pale face, dark hair, and square jaw of Lily's dead husband. Just as we were about to turn around and join the rest of his family, his eyes popped open and he winked.

A blood-curdling shriek filled the hushed room, and then I added my scream to the racket.

Raymond's little terrier, Pip, who had been sitting quietly at one end of the casket with a pink bow clipped on her head, yipped and yapped and charged at us, probably thinking she needed to ward off some terrible spirit about to invade her precious Raymond.

My arms flew up in the air. My silver hair clip popped open, releasing a cascade of crazy curls around my face.

Pip nipped at my ankles.

Lily crashed on to the thick, cushy carpet.

The room fell silent as I tried to make sense of what had happened.

All I could imagine was that Lily had just died from shock right in front of my eyes. Either that, or I had lost my mind. Or both, since the reality was too crazy to believe.

I crouched next to Lily and fanned her pale face with the program I'd grabbed on the way in. "Lily, don't you dare leave me" I ordered. "Come on, open those beautiful blue eyes. You're my best friend in all the world, and I need you to keep me sane, especially in this roomful of your in-laws."

I heard a snort above me. It was a familiar sound. One I'd heard more times than I could remember. The snort that belonged to Lily's almost ex-husband, Raymond, the dead guy who winked at us. A shiver of alarm zinged up my spine.

What was going on?

Lily moaned. I nearly fainted with relief and moved so she'd only be able to see me when her eyes opened. "What happened?" she mumbled.

My plan to shield Lily failed. I felt Ray's hot breath on my neck as he crouched next to me. Lily's eyes opened so wide I was afraid they might freeze into a fright mask and never close.

Pip wiggled close to Lily and licked her cheek.

"See, Lily?" Ray said, his voice actually tender. "Pip's thrilled to see you, too." Lily pushed herself to a sitting position, her cheeks regaining a bit of healthy pink glow. She pointed her finger at Ray. I truly expected to see daggers fly from that finger straight to Ray's heart, sending him back into that white casket he'd recently inhabited. "What the heck is going on?"

"Lily," Ray said in his fake soothing tone as he reached for her hand. She slapped him.

"You wouldn't answer any of my calls." His whiny voice told me something was up. This guy never begged for anything. He took what he wanted. "I was desperate to talk to you and stop this silly divorce you seem to be intent on carrying out."

"Silly? You think you can sweet talk me after what you did?" Lily pushed herself straighter as her spine seemed to grow a steel rod.

"I said I'm sorry." He even bowed his head a little.

I gagged. My blueberry muffin threatened to make a grand entrance. Again.

My head swiveled between Lily and Ray so fast I thought it might fall off. "Sorry?" I couldn't help but get involved. "If you hadn't put your, you know what, in you know where, we wouldn't be here."

The entire room fell silent. Even Pip sat down.

My hand flew to cover my big mouth. "Did I say that out loud?" I asked Lily.

She nodded.

I stood up. "Sorry folks. The show's over." I grabbed Lily's hand and pulled her up next to me. "Let's go. I'll treat you to my latest creation— my blueberry cordial. I think we could both use a shot."

With that, Lily and I, with our heads high, walked past Ray, past his family, past the whispers of, "Did you hear what she said?" We continued to march out the door and down the steps of the white-columned funeral home like the aggrieved widow Lily should have been, leaning on her bestie for support.

"Too bad all that money will stay in his bank account now," I said, steering Lily to the parking lot. I did my best to console her with my arm around her waist as we continued to my car.

And I meant it. I really wanted the best for my friend, even though I had very recently experienced a small pang of envy.

"Oh, Dani," she said with a shrug. "It's never been about the money for me. When I first met Ray, he was the sweetest, kindest guy I'd ever dated. It was love at first sight. But..."

I bit my tongue since I'd never seen that sweet,

kind side of Ray Lemay. He'd always had an ego the size of the ocean and a lust for money that seemed to rule his every action. But who was I to point any of that out to Lily? She'd finally discovered his betrayal when she found him in bed with her cousin. Of course, Ray shed some tears— fake I assumed— and promised Lily the moon, the stars, and a trip to Bali.

Lily had enough sense to walk out on him and serve him with divorce papers. After a little encouragement from moi of course, because sometimes your best friend needs more than a helping hand and silent support.

"But what?" I asked, hoping Lily would finish her thought.

"I never told you this because, well, you and Ray never seemed to hit it off."

"I won't argue with that." With my car idling, I asked, "Tell me what, Lil?"

"Ray kept a box full of cards and letters from all of his old flames. I told myself he was being sentimental, but now?" She tilted her head as if trying to solve a puzzle. "Now, I'm not sure what to think."

I decided staying silent, which was hard for me, was possibly the best course of action at the moment. I reached across the seat and squeezed her hand before I pulled away from the funeral home and headed to the Little Dog Diner.

I could feel her eyes on me as she said, "Thanks, Dani. I know I can always count on you. At least we have the diner— you, me, and Rose."

"Yes, I said," keeping my eyes on the traffic but feeling a warm flush at her reminder of our bond."

Until she added, "Ray always hated our arrangement."

"What?" I said, giving her a side eye? "Why? What business was it of his what our arrangement was? Er, is?" A little twang of nervousness clutched at my midsection. Was she about to share another tidbit I wasn't expecting?

I couldn't see the expression on her face when she said, "He thought I should own the building." But I could tell she had turned to me, her seatbelt stretching over the "appropriate" black widow's outfit I'd talked her into wearing. "Do you think Rose would sell it to me?"

"Sell you the diner?" The idea rendered me speechless, well almost. I'd sped the few miles across town, and now I pulled into the narrow strip between two properties owned by my grandmother, Rose Mackenzie: the Little Dog Diner and the historic brick building next door. She had connections in the Blueberry Bay Area, going back generations.

"Actually," Lily said, her voice trembling a bit. "Ray thinks I should own both properties."

My eyebrows hit my hairline. Of course, he does, that slimy real estate investor. "And why does Ray think that's what you should do, Lily? You do realize that Rose has her business in that historic building next to the diner. Do you know how old it is? What would she do with the Blueberry Bay Grapevine? And what about me? Would I have to move out of the apartment above the newspaper?"

This conversation was irritating me to no end. I turned to her and narrowed my eyes. "And why, all of a sudden, are you doing what Ray thinks is best for you?" I smelled something rotten in the air and I didn't like it.

Lily seemed to slink down in her seat. "I didn't think about all that." Was that an apology I heard in her meek voice? I'd take it. After all, she was my best friend.

"This is what I think, Lily." I slid out of my twenty-year-old Honda held together with duct tape. "Ray owns the building on the other side of the diner and my guess is he wants to gobble up all the prime real estate on this street for himself. If you're actually still talking to him, tell him he's crazy. Rose will never sell."

We entered the Little Dog Diner through the kitchen. "You first," I said to Lily as I opened the door. I didn't want her to see the expression on my face until I had a chance to get rid of the shock over her absurd suggestion. Sometimes, Lily and I were not on the same page, usually when Ray got himself involved in her life. Too bad the guy was still vertical.

With the diner closed on Monday's, I grabbed a bottle of my blueberry cordial and dragged Lily back outside and up the stairs to my apartment.

A double shot of cordial would help immensely, even if it was only ten in the morning. It was late enough for a drink somewhere, right? Besides, I suspected Lily was holding back a few more tidbits of information about Ray, and I needed to loosen her tongue.

Are you ready to read more? Buy or borrow *Mixing Up Murder* to continue the mystery today!

Get your copy at mollymysteries.com/LittleDogDiner

ABOUT MOLLY FITZ

While *USA Today bestselling* author Molly Fitz can't technically talk to animals, she and her three feline writing assistants have deep and very animated conversations as they navigate their days.

She lives with her child and their own private zoo somewhere in the wilds of Alaska. Molly will occasionally venture out for good food, great coffee, or to meet new animal friends.

Learn more about Molly and her books, and be sure to sign up for her newsletter at **www.Molly Mysteries.com**.

ALSO BY MOLLY FITZ

Learn more about Molly's collected works, so that you can decide which book you'd like to read next...

PET WHISPERER P.I.

Angie Russo just partnered up with Blueberry Bay's first ever talking cat detective. Along with his ragtag gang of human and animal helpers, Octo-Cat is determined to save the day... so long as it doesn't interfere with his schedule.

Start with book 1, ***Kitty Confidential***.

MERLIN'S MAGICAL MYSTERIES

Gracie Springs is not a witch... but her cat is. Now she must help to keep his secret or risk spending the rest of her life in some magical prison. Too bad trouble seems to find them at every turn!

Start with book 1, ***Merlin Takes a Familiar***.

PARANORMAL TEMP AGENCY

Tawny Bigford's simple life takes a turn for the magical when she stumbles upon her landlady's murder and is recruited by a talking black cat named Fluffikins to take over the deceased's role as the official Town Witch for Beech Grove, Georgia.

Start with book 1, ***Witch for Hire***.

THE MYSTERIES OF MOONLIGHT MANOR (WITH TRIXIE SILVERTALE)

Sydney Coleman has it all—until she doesn't. No sooner does she launch her bed and breakfast, than a trio of ghosts turn up oppose her at every turn. They insist she solve the murder of their mistress, but Sydney is desperate for cash. If she can't book some guests fast, her haunted mansion is utterly doomed.

Start with book 1, **Moonlight & Mischief**.

CONNECT WITH MOLLY

Sign up for my newsletter and get a special digital prize pack for joining, including an exclusive story, *Meowy Christmas Mayhem*, fun quiz, and lots of cat pictures!

Sign up: **MollyMysteries.com/subscribe**

Now, if you ever wished you could converse with cats, here's your opportunity! This is me officially inviting you into my whacky inner world as part of my Cozy Kitty Book Club.

For those who just can't get enough of my zany cat characters and their hapless humans, this book club will provide new content to devour and the chance to get to know my best author friends.

From exclusive stories, behind-the-scenes trivia to never-before-released bonus content, and monthly giveaways, there's a lot to love about the Cozy Kitty Book Club. Join today to find out what we're reading next!

Join: **MollyMysteries.com/club**